Shadow and Salvation

Faculty and Students of the Theological College of St. Van Helsing

Vanessa Knipe

BooksForABuck.com

2014

Contents

Shadows on the Wall

Nathaniel Trewithick staggered along until his hand caught on the next lamppost, a pyramid of light in these dark streets near St Paul's Cathedral. No tourists here searching for night life. He glanced around. Sodding traffic cones, never one around when you need one.

He took another swig from his hip flask. He should be sitting in a pub celebrating his pass into the sixth year, not fulfilling some stupid bet. It would be last orders and pub closing time before he finished this.

Maybe Paunchard would let him complete the bet tomorrow—not a chance, and he'd gloat.

There by that car! Well, not a traffic cone per se, but a police cone. It would have to do. He ambled over. Leaning on the back of the car with one hand, he picked up the cone—smaller than a standard traffic cone, much easier to carry. With the yellow plastic cone hooked under one arm he patted his pocket: good the camera was there.

Trewithick continued his drunken meander, plotting his revenge if Paunchard passed his fifth year exam.

Paternoster Square here he came: well, after he'd transacted more urgent business. He needed a quiet wall right now, any wall would do. He peered around. A cul-de-sac of Victorian redbrick houses called out to him. Setting his cone down, he reached for his fly, his mind divorced from what his body was about to do. Until, that is, the sign 'Amen Court' caught his eye. Quickly, he zipped up. Even drunk, he knew pissing against the house of the Dean of St Paul's Cathedral was a bad career move for a student of the Theological College of 'St Van Helsing'. He sniggered about the nickname as he continued his urgent quest. The tutors were trying to stamp on the name, but it had taken hold.

Away from lights, he found a quiet street with a drain. As he listened to the call of nature, he heard a voice and the sound of a large group of people coming his way. Argh! God was against him tonight.

"*He made darkness his secret place.*" Trewithick gathered the night around him like a cloak. Almost a misuse of Practical Theology but six pints of beer made stopping right now impossible.

All they saw was darkness, all they heard was the traffic crawling down Cheapside even this late at night. A siren howled, rushing to St Bartholomew's Hospital. The group walked past the end of his alley. He barely dared to breathe.

"And Amelia Dyer said to the guard, 'You'll be seeing me soon.' ..." the guide said.

Oh! It was a tourist Ghost Walk. Then they were gone.

With his business finished, Trewithick searched for his plastic cone. He still had to complete his bet and claim his pint of bitter. Oh yes, he'd left it by the Dean's house in Amen Court.

Darkness coiled around him. He admired the swirly patterns in his shadow. Why was his camouflage still hanging around? He shrugged, which sent him stumbling for the nearest wall. With one hand leaning on the bricks he shook his head, trying to clear out the fuzz.

Walking a little more steadily, he followed after the Ghost Walk group. The darkness flowed around him like an oil slick in the air.

Stopping at Amen Court, he retrieved his cone. It was time to invade Paternoster Square and cap the Shepherd statue, take a photograph and thump Paunchard for handing out such a stupid bet.

The darkness froze, as if it were a startled animal. It surged down Amen Court.

"Hey, get back here! You're my darkness." He pointed in front of his feet, as if he were training a dog.

The shadow ignored him, oozing like fresh tarmac along the road. Okay, something was odd.

With his cone tucked under his arm, he crept—well, even he had to admit he *staggered along* less noisily—towards the disturbance in the natural balance. Or as he liked to call it *The Force*. He sniggered at this joke, and then remembered he was being sneaky.

The tour guide stood at the old wall of Newgate Jail. "Back in the reign of Henry III a famine struck London. The inmates of Newgate Jail were left to starve. During these days a scholar was imprisoned on a charge of ... Sorcery."

The guide paused and shared a conspiratorial glance with his tour group of five people. The two women snuggled up to their menfolk. The odd man out aimed his camera, taking a photograph of the brick wall. Trewithick leaned against a lamppost. Why did his camouflage like *this* group?

"Not long into his incarceration, the felons killed and ate the scholar in their desperation. Within days, a huge black dog, foul-smelling with eyes of fire and jaws that dripped with blood prowled the jail in the dead of the night. It caught and ripped apart two of the inmates before the remaining felons killed their jailors to escape. They scattered the length of the country. It did them no good. The black dog hunted them down wherever they hid. When the murder of the Scholar/Sorcerer had been avenged, the black dog returned to the jail and stalked the corridors, preceded by its stench, on nights when a condemned person was due to hang the next morning."

Trewithick's Darkness slid up the wall radiating an odd eagerness.

"And even though they demolished the jail in 1902 often a black shadow crawls down the wall. *Fiat!*"

The drains around here must be blocked up. Mist rising from the grating at his feet made the six pints in Trewithick's stomach a major regret.

"Oh Lord, heal me for my bones are vexed." His stomach settled.

Wailing and rattling circled the court, like a singer squawking to a xylophone accompaniment. Darkness slid down the wall.

The Guide smirked as one man aimed his camera. He lowered it, mouth wide open in amazement as glowing red eyes appeared in the center of the shadow.

The younger woman screamed and pointed. Her boyfriend wrapped his arms around her, staring in horrified delight at the light show.

The older woman clasped her hand over her nose and mouth. The Camera Man tucked his elbow over his nose as he attempted to aim his camera again. As the tour group backed away the older woman vomited over the pavement. Her partner hauled her away from the stench.

The Guide stared at his hands, then at the coalescing beast. "*Vado!*" he shouted.

The shadow refused to be banished. Legs formed out of its substance.

The malfunctioning camouflage had mixed up with an illusion spell from a Sorcerer posing as a Tour Guide. Trewithick ran a hand through his hair: time to put a stop to this.

"Let the wicked perish through their own imaginations."

Trewithick had intended the black dog to attack the Sorcerer but as he planned his working the younger woman flung her arms around her boyfriend, burying her nose in his chest. Instead of focusing on the sorcerer and the Black Dog, Trewithick wished he had that much lush flesh pressed against him.

The working circled the court and finding nothing else to hit, slammed into Trewithick. Backlash agony forced him to his knees. Gasping for breath, he watched the Shadow grow a body out of the evil-smelling mist. This was no time to be out for the count.

The guide-sorcerer backed away, staring in horror at his creation. He sprinted towards the exit of the court.

"Stop!"

Trewithick grabbed the nearest thing, his traffic cone, and hurled it after the sorcerer. It spun awkwardly, but he had lost none of his rugger arm. The point of the cone slammed into the back of the Sorcerer's knee. He sprawled on the street howling.

Still groggy from his own curse, Trewithick clambered to his feet. The tour group stood watching the display in fascination.

"Run!" He stood in front of the innocent bystanders. "Your guide went that way."

With this much power flying around Amen Court, the college would scramble a rapid response team, but it was up to him to keep the beast off the civilians until the top guys got here.

Without his staff to use as a focus, he held up a hand to the beast, now fully formed as advertised with blood-dripping jowls. *"Go ye cursed into the fire everlasting."*

Flames rose up around the beast. The tarmac bubbled and melted in the heat. What was wrong with his workings this evening? That was banishment, not fire summoning. The eyes of the evil critter picked up more fire from the heat of his spell.

The tour group applauded.

"Get out of here!" he shouted over his shoulder. Until they left he was stuck here, but they acted like he was part of the ghost tour.

The black dog stalked the tourists.

Trewithick swung his hand back, as if he held a night stick. "*I will smite down his foes before his face.*"

The black dog skidded backwards as he slammed his empty hand at it. Sure, it bumped into the old wall of Newgate Jail but without much force behind that blow. His mojo had taken a holiday—had the demon from his last fight cursed him, or something?

That blow attracted the Dog's full attention to Trewithick. The Beast paced forwards; its foaming tongue hanging between razor-sharp teeth.

He had intended to hold the critter until the big guns arrived, but now he had a full demon to fight. And he had no weapon.

Trewithick crouched, prepared to ram a fist in a burning eye. He'd passed year five, dying right now would be so feeble.

Think, you idiot. Thought would be a lot easier if he hadn't been intent on killing all his brain cells in the pub earlier.

Identify weaknesses. Large black dogs with fiery eyes and fangs dripping blood didn't tend to have weaknesses.

Hold it, since this creature was a combination of Trewithick's camouflage spell and the sorcerer's illusion then if Trewithick banished his darkness the combination should fall apart. Not a good idea but it was the one that floated to the top of his alcohol sodden brain.

The Black Dog crouched. Its tail held high and stiff. Its growl rumbled through Trewithick's boots. Despite his failures, he had to try because the people behind had yet to budge.

Gritting his teeth, he stood tall and spread his hands. "*They shall walk in the Light of Thy countenance.*"

The Black Dog launched at Trewithick.

Trewithick's erratic skill exploded into a glowing sunburst. Daylight filled the street—far brighter than he'd expected. The creature slammed into Trewithick's expanding aura.

Paws first then slathering jowls, the shadow burnt away. The last things that fell to the ground were the glowing eyes, as the spark died it left behind two lumps of coal. A breeze from Eden filled the Court and purged the stench of the beast.

All his strength drained away with that one show of power. As the bright light faded he fell to his hands and knees gasping for breath.

The tour group applauded.

Four college tutors ran into Amen Court headed by the Watcher, Mr. Werlow.

"Trewithick! What happened here?" Mr. Werlow demanded.

"Nothing worked." Trewithick complained to his elder in the College.

Another tutor, Mr. Loversall, sheathed his sword and tucked a hand under Trewithick's shoulder, hauling him to his feet.

"Why did you pass me?" Trewithick said. "Everything went wrong."

"But you stayed to fight anyway—you mad, boy?" Mr. Loversall said.

"What! And let the people get eaten!"

"And you believe you shouldn't be in the sixth." Mr. Loversall sniffed Trewithick's breath. "You been drinking, boy? Don't deny it, you smell like a brewery."

Trewithick studied his feet. "I had a few."

"Work and pleasure don't mix, boy," Mr. Loversall said. "I'm surprised anything happened at all."

Two other masters took the tour group aside as Trewithick remembered the Sorcerer. He scoured the Court. The traffic cone lay alone, on its side with no downed Sorcerer to hand over to the big guns.

"The tour guide got away! He called an illusion, but it was real."

"I expect he'd used the spell too many times in the same place," Mr. Werlow said.

"The tour group wouldn't run away." Trewithick decided not to mention his darkness.

Mr. Loversall tidied the traffic cone to one side. "Back to college and sleep off your load, son. You'll need an exorcism in the morning for that nasty curse."

Trewithick flushed. No way would he admit he'd cursed himself.

"We need to stop annoying the Dean and Chapter of St Paul's."
Mr. Werlow waved a hand at the twitching curtains.

In silence Mr. Loversall marched Trewithick along, keeping him
upright by sheer strength of arm. On Cheapside, a man kicked at a
wheel clamp fitted on his car. Trewithick hung his head; he had
taken the police cone from behind that car, one more thing that was
his fault this evening. Trewithick sneaked another glance at the
benighted motorist. He held his crumpled parking ticket as if he
would throw it on the ground and dance on it.

Trewithick shrugged off Loversall. "That's the Sorcerer who
summoned the Black Dog."

Mr. Werlow had the tour guide in an arm lock before the man
protested his innocence. "It is an offense, under Department of the
Environment regulations, to summon a dangerous beast or spirit in a
built up area."

"That's the first time it happened," the Sorcerer said.

Behind them, one of the other tutors explained to the tour group
they had watched special effects for a new movie, and sorry for the
inconvenience, but they had to confiscate their cameras for
copyright reasons.

The Skull Beneath the Skin

Over the top of his paper, Dunkley saw Trewithick trudging up the station path, favoring his right hip. He let his hiking staff support him like an exhausted Norse god heading out for Ragnarok, only with a better wardrobe of course. The current waistcoat drowned out the sun.

Trewithick hailed him. "Hi there! Did you do anything fun over the summer vacation?"

Dunkley thought over the holiday he'd spent with his father's cousin at Caisteal an Dunkley.

***

Dunkley opened his messenger bag. The book he'd brought from college sat inside along with a packed lunch his cousin's wife had ordered for his 'day trip to the seaside'.

"And a nice day, you'll have for it, Alasdair," Cousin Màiri had said. "Don't worry if you're late for supper, cook has decreed we're having salad since it's to be so hot today."

She was right about the day; the sun burned through the hazy cloud that had gathered overnight, to the point where he was wishing he'd brought sunscreen—a Sassenach's product unheard of and unneeded in the Highlands.

For a moment, he smelled smoke. He laid a palm on the ground. Still soggy from yesterday, and the day before, and the week before that, there'd be no burning moor today. The smoke must come from a chimney on one of the cottages he'd passed to reach this place. This was going to be the one day in the year with no rain.

Better for the book though; he opened it at the flint knapping page. Weighting it open with rocks, he studied the knife making process. Now that he was home, sometimes it was difficult to think in the English the book was written in. He traced the lines with his fingertip.

Just one more year at the college in London, then he would be home and he could sort out the mess his father had left of the Estate. He'd had the right idea but chose the wrong method.

First Dunkley would need some flint. He studied the photographs of the best type of flint. Leaving the bag and the book where he'd set them, he tucked his torch in the waistband of his kilt. He scrambled over to the pit and stared into it. There were few enough ancient flint mines in Scotland. He'd driven to the 'seaside' in Aberdeenshire for this one.

The stone edge of the pit was padded with dry, brown moss. He clambered down. A kilt was a far more sensible piece of kit than the trousers he wore in London. It left his legs free for climbing, no tight restrictions on movement. He imagined trying to sell the idea to his effete friend Trewithick and snorted.

Reaching the bottom, he switched on his torch and searched the area. His boots flattened the verdant moss. A number of tunnels ran into the rock. Picking one at random, he hunched over and walked deeper in. The chill was marked after the sun up there. There by the wall, he spied a chunk missed by those ancient miners. Hefting it, he looked around, warily. That was almost too easy. Spotting nobody, he headed out into the light. With the torch back in his waistband and a chunk of flint in his sporran, he climbed up to the daylight world.

He switched on his battery-powered radio and settled on the rock. Wouldn't want to miss the rugby—a friendly between Scotland A and the Wallabies.

He tied back his shoulder length hair into the ponytail that was the fashion at college with both students and masters. With the radio commentary on low, he lit a cigarette and slid his case into the pocket of the waistcoat he wore over a tee shirt. Comfortable, he worked at the stone knife necessary for the ritual he intended. He struck the flint with a granite hammer stone gathered from his home.

"What are you doing?"

Dunkley jumped, the cigarette fell out of his mouth. He stamped on it, despite the wet conditions—he was no firebug. Intent on his work, he'd failed to notice the approach of young woman, not much older than his own twenty three.

He switched off the radio. "I'm making a flint athame."

"For what purpose?" The woman knelt beside him to study his work. Her shabby jeans protected her knees from the stones around here. Her embroidered blouse was in retro fashion; Dunkley remembered his mother had worn similar style blouses, though never once the embroidery frayed like on this girl's top. The young woman spoke with an English accent—again like his mother, though his mother had learned *Gaidhlig* in self-defense.

"To learn how." The crisp Sassenach words from his life in London slid onto his tongue. "What other reason might I have?"

"You can't learn that from a book."

"There's no one to teach me."

She sat cross-legged. "Hand it over. Flint knapping was taught in the first year of my archaeology degree."

"Are you sure you want to sit there? That ground is damp." He slid over to leave a bit of space on his rock.

"This bit of heather is quite dry, thank you." She reached out a hand for his work.

Dunkley handed over the flint and hammerstone. "I'm Alasdair Dunkley. Are you on a dig?"

"I'm studying the flint quarry. I came to confront a vandal." She ground down the edge of the flint with the hammer stone. "You need to prepare the edges, otherwise it snaps as you shape the blade. Antler is the best hammer for working flint. It finishes the edges, nice and sharp. I'm Annelise Coulton."

Her shoulder length hair hung over her shoulders as she worked the edges of the stone. He leaned closer to watch her delicate fingers work the flint.

"Were you not afraid to approach a potential site-wrecker?"

"Should I be?" She jerked her head up.

He stared into her cool blue eyes. "I'm a Theology student."

"Plenty of rocks if I need to drop one on your head." She grinned: it was infectious. "Here, prepare the edges, like I showed you."

She handed the tools over. Dunkley attempted to copy her hand action.

Annelise giggled. "Not like that." She reached around from behind him and took his hands in hers to guide his movements. "See, now?"

She smelled of the earth around here and the touch of her hand caressed his like a silken glove.

"Like this?" Dunkley leaned back a little into her hold and her breasts stroked his shoulder. Her hair rubbed on his cheek; it smelled as if she washed it in rose water. Pretty enough for an afternoon's company, especially as Cousin Màiri had made it clear he was to 'break no hearts on the Estate with his loose London ways'.

"It's a little better. You need more practice." She watched for a moment longer, and then released him. She held out her hands. "Next you must thin the blade."

Dunkley handed the flint and hammer stone over. He enjoyed watching her concise movements as she struck the top of the stone. The tip of her tongue edged out as she concentrated—like a cat purring.

She lifted off a flake. "I've taken off about 4mm."

Dunkley took back the tools and attempted the strike. Getting it right was important—the tools shaped the work. Cousin Màiri and her husband were good custodians and had improved the land, but without power it was slow going. He intended his Estate to be perfect again. And *he* would be the right tool.

"Are you from around here?" Annelise asked.

"Och, no." Dunkley lifted the hammer stone for another strike. "I live in the Highlands. I needed flint and we're on granite."

"You've got the hang of it now." Annelise rocked back on her heels preparing to rise.

"Do you want to share my picnic?" Dunkley tried to postpone her departure. "My cousin Màiri packed enough for an army."

She glanced back at the quarry.

"Annelise!" A man's voice shouted out of the pit. "Where are you?"

"I've got to go." All the joy left her face as she jumped to her feet. Raising her voice she added, "I'm coming professor."

She scrambled away. Her eyes locked onto his as she scrambled over the edge. *Help me.*

Dunkley set the half-formed knife onto the ground. He crept over to the top of the pit and lay to peer over the edge.

In the depths was a raggedy man with gray straggly hair, not a professor type at all, more your standard hedge warlock, a wannabe black sorcerer: scruffy, dressed in black, failed, old. Movies that depicted these petty evil types as suave and debonair had never seen the reality: pitiful. A true Black Sorcerer was a monster—he knew from experience. But experience is a great teacher, even from a monster.

"Why did you go out?" the warlock demanded with a hand raised above a kneeling Annelise. "You disturbed him. I was enjoying listening to the rugby."

"He came into the mine." Annelise cringed away from the warlock's falling hand. "I was trying to discover what he wanted."

"*Thou shalt show us wonderful things,*" Dunkley whispered.

As he suspected, magical bonds linked the warlock and Annelise.

"He wants what is mine. No one else will ever have you." The warlock hauled Annelise down the second tunnel on the right.

Someone as beautiful as Annelise should not be bound against her will. Once there had been a lady bound to a monster. And he had failed to save her. He was older now. Dunkley prepared to slay any number of dragons for this maiden. She might be grateful.

He pushed away from the edge and walked back to his chosen work space. His bare knee brushed the ground cover, Annelise had found the one spot of dry heather on the moor to sit on—an old dead plant.

Tidying away the book and radio into his messenger bag, he tucked the half-finished knife into his sporran. He would continue working it later. Despite Annelise's nonchalance about vandals, Dunkley's belongings would be safer with him rather than left in the open for an indefinite time period. He hooked the bag crosswise over his chest.

With his torch stuffed down his waistband, he laid down at the pit edge again and listened. Dunkley kept patience until he no longer heard their echoing footsteps. He slid over the edge. He climbed into the pit faster than a monkey, bag bouncing on his hip. All those hours in the gym at college paid off.

He tiptoed over to the tunnel they had taken into the earth. Listening hard, he heard the warlock's voice. He waited until he heard nothing but his own heartbeat. Having finished his fourth year at the Theological College was he ready to take on a warlock steeped in villainy for more years than Dunkley had birthdays? He should go back to his car and find a payphone. Call in a college senior.

But then it would be the senior who rescued Annelise, the darkness of the tunnel whispered to him. *The senior would have her gratitude.*

No one had rescued his mother from his beast of a father. The clan whispered how she brought out the beast in him by acting the victim. When improving the Estate with magic had failed, his father had bound a rich bride to him.

The pretty locket his mother had worn all the time was a control charm created by her husband.

Black sorcery would never bring good, but at college they taught him the white. Dunkley intended to learn as much as possible up to the end of his fifth year coming up. After that he would leave the college and cleanse the fetid pools of darkness, chasing all witches from Dunkley lands.

Why he was in the mine?

A terrified scream burst out of the tunnel.

It was the scream made by his mother, falling down the stairs; the cry of a woman for whom death is the better option.

Annelise.

No one deserved to be raped and murdered. He pounded along in the darkness, determined to reach Annelise. His bag scraped against the rock walls and he slammed into a barrier.

He bit back his groan. Common sense swept over him. If he charged around like rutting bull they'd hear him. Doing this rescue blind would help no one.

He stretched out his arms. On either side of the narrow tunnel Stone Age miners had left grooves as they gouged away the rock with their stone and antler tools. Closing his eyes so he could pretend the darkness didn't blind him, he edged around the column of rock he had rammed.

He groped along the tunnel. The darkness urged haste, who knew what horrors Annelise suffered for her crime of talking to another man.

She had to obey the warlock with all those spells binding her. She was not to know Dunkley was in training to deal with this sort of trouble, but she'd asked for his help anyway.

Echoes muddled the whispers traveling through the tunnel

"*His ears are open to their prayers,*" Dunkley whispered.

"I need a new girl, new girl, new girl. Soon. Soon. This one won't last much longer, longer, not much longer."

Dunkley opened his eyes. That had to be the warlock. The pitch was higher, but Annelise would have no reason to say those things.

He stayed his next step.

Perhaps more people than the warlock and his slave hid in this mine. If that were the case then he would need back-up. Was there anyone close? He had no reason to know. Scottish locals dealt with their own witches without calling in the intruder Church of England.

Dunkley dithered over the pros of returning to daylight.

A stray drift of air brought rose scent from her hair to his nose; it clung to his tee shirt from where she had leant against him.

Sobs drifted down the tunnel.

What was he doing? Annelise needed help now. That voice was talking about killing her and getting a 'new girl'. He needed to scout the situation, and if possible get Annelise free. He had to ensure her safety before phoning for help to take down the warlock.

The sobs urged him to run, but his patience forced caution. Ahead he saw light. Pressed tight to the rock wall, he edged along the tunnel.

At the end of the passageway a room had been carved out of the rock. Bare light bulbs illuminated it. Where did they steal the electricity from? His nostrils flared in disgust at the smell of human habitation in an enclosed space as he studied the room. Below a dais carved out of the rock, Annelise lay on the floor as if she had been flung there. On the dais stood a stone altar decorated with a heavy-breasted mother goddess figurine—a Stone Age Venus of Aberdeenshire. Fit right in with a Stone Age flint mine.

Sobs shook Annelise's back. Ignoring her, the warlock pottered around putting a kettle over a fire that had a chimney. That must have been the smoke Dunkley smelled on the moor; it pleased him to have that mystery cleared up.

"I haven't heard a radio since last year. I'd be more content if you let me have one pleasure."

Just like a standard abuser to blame the victim. It made the victim blame themselves harder. He'd watched it with his mother—before his father had murdered her.

The warlock tossed an empty beer can at Annelise. It bounced off her shoulder. She sat up and wiped her eyes on the grubby sleeve of her blouse.

"Did you even get his cigarettes?"

Annelise handed over Dunkley's silver cigarette case with ARD engraved on the front. Dunkley patted his waistcoat pocket. Her pickpocket abilities were faultless.

The warlock snatched the case. It smelled enough bad down here; how the warlock put up with the stench was beyond him. The chimney provided limited ventilation but he lit a cigarette anyway. Maybe he wanted to drown out the stink.

Only two people were in the room after all. This was going to be so easy. He would distract the warlock while he got Annelise to safety. Call in a senior practitioner to do the tidy-up, problem sorted.

Dunkley retrieved his radio from his messenger bag. He switched it on and the commentator's voice rang out through the cave.

The warlock spun and raised his hand. "*Detineo!*"

Dunkley's legs stuck fast to the rock. "*Let not the hand of the Ungodly strike me down.*"

The warlock laughed. "You're one of them? She likes their failures. You won't last two minutes against her. *Habeo non habeor.*"

The hold on Dunkley's legs increased.

"I was one of them. Up to my fifth year," the warlock said.

Dunkley shook his head. "You were never one of us!"

The warlock sneered. "*He made darkness his secret place.*"

Dark gathered around him like a cloak. Behind him, Annelise stared around the room with a puzzled expression. "Professor? Where are you?"

"That's not true!"

"Oh! An idealist, like I used to be." Self-loathing transfigured the warlock's face. "I dreamt of driving witches from our bonny land."

"I am not like you!"

The warlock studied the clan tartan of Dunkley's kilt. "And why otherwise would a good Highlands boy join the Church of England. Witches are natural to Scotland—it's the Church that's the infestation."

He didn't have to listening to this. Dunkley thrust the radio up. *"Listen to the Word of the Lord."*

Anger and terror poured strength into the working. The warlock lost focus on his spells holding Dunkley and fastened his attention on the radio commentary. Able to move his legs again, Dunkley lowered the radio to the floor. As he set it down, the warlock crouched ever closer to the speaker until he lay on the floor with his ear pressed right against the grill.

Dunkley shook off the last of the holding spell. He snatched his cigarette case from the warlock's hand and stuffed it in his pocket. That had been close. Letting the warlock speak first was a mistake. He'd better not let happen again. What had the warlock been talking about when …?

"Kill him now." Annelise stabbed her finger at the warlock.

A red rage ran through Dunkley's head. He raised the dirk from his sock above his head. He hung over the warlock who lay helpless on the floor. Now would be a good time to strike.

Imagination supplied the blood spreading out over the floor. What had the warlock done to her, to make her so vengeful?

"Kill him." Annelise's voice took on the hissing of a serpent.

I don't kill helpless people. I've never killed anyone. He shook his head. "That's not how we work." He tucked the knife back into his sock and grabbed her arm. "Let's get out of here. The College team will deal with him."

"He should die. I'll kill him if you're too chicken." She snatched for the dirk, but Dunkley caught her fast with one arm.

"We are leaving here now." His best Laird Dunkley voice; peasants obey or there will be consequences. He hauled on her arm as he walked towards the tunnel.

"Wait!" Annelise tugged on his arm. "The statue. We need that. It's unique in England. They've only ever been found on the continent before this."

Because it would keep her calm, he lifted the statue of the Earth Goddess off the altar and tucked it under his arm. "Now, let's go."

They entered the dark tunnel leaving the warlock glued to the radio. What had the warlock meant when he said …?

Annelise wrapped her arm around Dunkley's waist. "You rescued me," she whispered in his ear. The scent of roses washed over him.

His spine straightened as his chest expanded with pride. His head banged on the low ceiling. "Oww."

"I can kiss it better."

That sent more ideas running down his spine, but he kept hunched over. "Later."

She nibbled at his ear in the dark, but made no further advances. Up ahead, the light grew as they approached the pit. Annelise urged him forward.

Something smelled bad around here. Annelise had better take a bath before her promised reward. She carried the stench of the cave with her.

When they had met above ground she had smelled clean and fresh like the countryside. Now her skin peeled away as her face rotted off. Two teeth fell out as he watched. He snatched his hand away from her arm and reeled towards the light.

"You're dead!"

"I'm not." Annelise's grin was hideous as half her cheek splatted like rotten meat on the ground. Maggots ate through the flesh.

There was no echo from Annelise's voice. It rang in his head. 'She' that's what the warlock had said. The bonds ran the other way not from the warlock to Annelise, but Annelise controlled the warlock. Still carrying the statue, Dunkley backed out of the tunnel into the daylight that fell as far as the pit floor.

"What's wrong, Alasdair?" Annelise stepped into the light. Her remaining skin fell away and her rag-clothed skeleton broke up, chinking to the cave floor like a glockenspiel.

"Oh God!"

"What's wrong, Alasdair?"

"What?" Dunkley spun around. Who was saying that?

Laughter echoed around the pit. Grit crumbled in his hand. As sunlight hit the clay statue it cracked and splintered, disintegrating into sand. Bringing it out of the Flint mine had destroyed the immaculate preservation. What was happening? A wind blew around the pit and statue exploded into dust that swirled up.

"Finally, I'm free. No more eating women to keep up my strength up."

Wind whirled around Alasdair. It pulled at his hair, untying the pony tail. The wind ripped at his clothes. He hunkered down, covering his head with his hands as the whirlwind spiraled down. Rocks flew around the small pit crashing into the walls.

"And you, Alasdair, will be my consort."

"No!" he shouted into the wind.

It stopped. The flying rocks hung in the air around him. He stood in a small circle of calm. The sun darkened as clouds gathered above the pit.

"What did you say?"

"I said, 'No'. What, are ye deaf?" Dunkley lifted his head. An image of an Earth Goddess, made from swirling dust, formed in front of him.

"You bow before me. I was captured by creeping people who sought to steal parts of the earth. They made me stay in the ground to give them air as they worked at their theft."

Dunkley would not worship before this creature. He pushed to his feet. "I do not bow before you."

"Really?" The whirlwind spread out, touching him. It pushed against his chest but he refused to give ground. It tugged at his clothes and hair. Long strands of brown hair joined the dust and stones in the whirlwind.

"I do not bow before you."

"I can give you what you want, Alasdair. I can give you the power you need."

Dunkley stood his ground as the whirlwind retracted. The air filled with the scent of roses. Annelise stood before him in a beam of sunlight that broke through the thunder clouds. She was as beautiful as walking through the dew at dawn. The world spun around him.

She might be English but she was more than a match for the clan, not like his mother. Why had he thought Annelise was quick game? She would make a fine Lady Alasdair, and Lady Dunkley once his father was dead. She stepped towards him, her eyes wide open in amazement as she stared at him.

"Just take me," Annelise whispered. "Then you'll have the power to make your lands grow again."

He had never met a more wonderful woman in the whole world.

She was right; here was the power he needed. The Dunkley Estate would be rich again.

Her lips touched his and her arms wrapped around his neck. He caught her in a strong embrace.

"Annelise," he whispered. "I love you."

"Of course you do."

He lowered her to the mossy ground. She pulled him down to her lips as he unbuttoned her blouse. A delicate tongue explored his mouth as he pushed aside a bone to sit beside her. He suckled at her exposed breast.

Bone.

He pushed the shirt from her shoulders. Why did the word bother him? He unfastened her jeans, hands trembling with anticipation. He slid them over her hip bones and straddled her thin waist.

His mouth explored her body.

Bone.

"Alasdair, you rescued me. I belong to you." Annelise arched up to kiss him. The wind-borne scent of roses surrounded him.

"I worship you." His lips moved against hers.

He frowned. No he didn't worship her. He lifted his head to examine her face. She stared up into his eyes. She smiled, her lips curving up like a scimitar.

A pillow of bones and dead moss framed her face. The bones belonged to Annelise, she was dead. So how was he kissing her? He sat up.

"Thou hast fallen in love with unrighteousness."

"What did you say, Alasdair?"

The flesh melted away from bones again. He had been kissing a skull. He had … oh God!

He scuttled away from her, his arse scrapping the ground. His kilt fell over his withered ardor. The bones crawled after him. Her skeletal arm moved without the need for muscle. Bony fingers clutched at his ankle. Above him the wind howled with laughter. He reached the pit wall and used to it get to his feet.

All the moss in here was dead. It had been green when he dropped from the daylight world. The whirlwind sucked life out of everything to create the illusion of a living being.

How old was the warlock?

Dunkley stared at his hands. How much of his life had the creature stolen?

"What's wrong Alasdair? I can give you everything you desire."

Tears of terror ran down his cheeks as the whirlwind coiled down and re-clothed the bones with flesh. "I don't need you."

Annelise held out her arms. "Alasdair, I can be alive again if you love me."

"No!" He held an arm over his eyes to hide her delicate beauty. The roses smelled like they had fallen months ago and fermented in a puddle of dog-shit.

"Love me, darling." She crowded up against him. The curves of her body pressed against him. He leaned his head away from her tempting lips. "Me or no one."

"No!" He thrust her away.

She laughed, like a summer breeze through the trees. "You are mine, Alasdair, to toy with as I please."

Red fury blinded his sight. He was the next Laird Dunkley—no toy of a succubus.

He scrabbled in his sporran and pulled out the half-made flint knife. With his face averted he sprang at her. *"When the wicked, even mine enemies and foes, came on me to eat up my flesh, they stumbled and fell."*

He rammed the flint knife between the ribs of the animated corpse.

Flesh dissolved into light and blew away as dust, exposing the dry bone. The mouth of the skeleton opened as the creature of air attempted escape. The slice of solid earth jammed between the ribs bound the creature to the dead body. Dunkley slid along the wall of the pit, his breath sobbing.

The bones tumbled like dominos to the ground.

"NO!" the creature screamed. A puff of dust as the bone crumpled to the stone. The whirlwind vanished. The thunder clouds passed out to sea without dropping their load. The world was still. Above him, birds sang, calling him into the daylight world. The summer breeze whispered, "No."

He saw his mother falling down the stairs, as his father stood at the top certain he owned her and could do as he pleased with her—including kill her.

Tears burned Dunkley's cheeks. The Annelise he had met had never existed. He hadn't killed a real woman. He wasn't his father.

Half-blinded by his tears Dunkley scrambled up the sides of the pit. The dead moss and heather spread further from the pit now. As dead as parts of the Estate that his father had sucked dry with his sorcery.

At the top he stood, gazing down. He'd been cock-sure and the succubus nearly caught him—the way it had caught that former student of the college, now a warlock. A man who had left at year five, the way Dunkley had intended to.

That creature called to the darkness in him. He would never be safe to hold power without the College watching him. Màiri worked miracles without being a witch. The Estate didn't need another warlock-Laird like his father.

Dunkley's hands shook. He reached into his pocket for his cigarette case. Black fingerprints tarnished the bright silver of the case from where the warlock had held it: only the touch of real evil tarnished pure metal. He flung the silver case as far away from him as possible; it fell into the heather. He scrubbed his hands on the tough tartan of his kilt.

The tarnish stained his fingertips.

***

Dunkley folded his paper and tucked it into a pocket of his coat. The headline showed over the edge. Serial Killer Caught in Scottish Flint Mine. According to the paper (full story on page seven) he had been living with the bodies of four victims.

"Did you do anything interesting?" Trewithick asked again as Dunkley slung his rucksack over a shoulder.

"Nothing to speak of. I learnt how to make a flint knife." *Nothing? Oh, Annelise.* He had read her obituary in the paper, after the police had found the bodies due to an anonymous tip-off. The elemental had copied many of her mannerisms. "What about you?"

Trewithick grinned like the sun coming out. "You know that huge Air Elemental they've got stashed under Stone Henge? Well, it was playing up again. A plague of grasshoppers clogged up the army's tanks on the Salisbury Plain training ground ..." He took a packet from his shirt pocket. "Cigarette?"

"Ah! No thanks. I quit." Dunkley stuffed his hands in his jeans' pockets.

Dark Lord

Even in the middle of a fight, Dunkley noticed when Trewithick burst into the gymnasium. Perhaps Trewithick still thought of Dunkley as the weedy eleven-year-old who had arrived at public school fourteen years ago.

Dunkley sent a trickle of strength into the prayers inscribed on his hiking stick. With the prayers activated, he thwacked his sixth year opponent in the diaphragm.

The man staggered back, using his staff as a prop. "How did you get into the sixth year, Dark Lord?"

"Och, you're a big man! I subvert a tutor into passing me and you dare take me on." Dunkley followed his advantage with a blow aimed at ffalkenham's head.

ffalkenham whipped his staff up and slammed Dunkley's hiking stick to the floor. "You call me a coward?"

Dunkley yanked his stick away. "Ambushing a practice bout— that's not cowardly?" Sweat trickled down his back as he swung again for the side of ffalkenham's head.

"Like your puny rod will withstand pure oak." Using his oaken staff, ffalkenham swept aside the hiking stick with a strike meant to bend the light-weight aluminum pole. His mouth dropped open in surprise as the hiking stick remained undented after the force of his blow.

The prayer Dunkley had painted on the blue metallic paint—in blue metallic paint—made the stick as solid as oak, and spread the blow so Dunkley was hardly jarred by the attack. The aluminum pole hummed as it dissipated the energy.

"Your quaint English oaken staff." Maybe he was cheating, but Dunkley didn't believe in fair play when it came to the creatures he and his fellow Church Officers had to fight. It was a shame one of his fellow trainee Officers had decided to pick a fight.

ffalkenham came back to college this year full of stories to tell his gang of cheerleaders about the 'Black' Dunkleys.

He pointed his staff at Dunkley. *The Lord shall root out all deceitful lips.*

No! Using practical theology against a fellow apprentice was wrong. Dunkley's mouth dropped open as he watched the incoming working. He had no defense prepared. He skittered behind the wooden vaulting horse; a smell of burning leather drifted after him as the spell impacted.

"Stop, you idiot!" Dunkley hissed.

"Idiot yourself. Returning to the college." Beyond common sense, ffalkenham rounded the vaulting horse. *"Thou shalt bruise them with a rod of iron and break them in pieces like a potter's vessel."*

Dunkley staggered from the pounding on his undefended ribcage. He stumbled over a low-beam balance bar. Crashing to the floor, the air whooshed out of his lungs. Black spots swirled before his eyes.

He shook his head to clear it. Two tutors had joined Trewithick at his vigil near the entrance—including his own master, Mr. Werlow. Everyone saw Dunkley upended over the balance bar; at least he was in London, wearing jogging pants rather than his kilt.

"Defend yourself, Dunkley," Werlow said.

ffalkenham lunged, his staff raised to strike.

Dunkley rolled as the oaken staff slammed into the floor where his head had been.

"That thy foot may be dipped in the blood of thine enemies."

Behind him there was an almighty thump and clattering but Dunkley rolled until he hit one of the wooden climbing frames. He used the bars to haul himself to his feet. He brushed aside a lock of hair fallen from his pony tail and sticking to his sweaty face.

Werlow and Mr. Loversall helped ffalkenham to his feet. Loversall inspected a bruise forming across ffalkenham's forehead from where he hit the low-beam bar when he skidded on the suddenly slick polished wood floor. He tried to brush the tutor away but Werlow twisted him into an arm lock.

Dunkley sagged in relief; it was over.

"You know," Loversall said. "We haven't had a no holds barred fight in decades."

Werlow eased back on his grip on ffalkenham.

"Sirs …!" Trewithick trotted over to join the older members of the Inner Circle.

"No more protection. Let's find out what our sixth years can do," Werlow said. "I'm interested in the staying power of that new-fangled staff of Dunkley's."

Ice ran through Dunkley's stomach. Damn them, they were enjoying this.

"Trewithick!" Werlow pointed to the end of the gymnasium.

Trewithick dragged his feet but complied.

ffalkenham shook his arms as Werlow released him. He picked up his oaken staff and flicked off imaginary dust, sliding his hands down its polished length and running his fingers over the prayers carved into its side by his family predecessors in the College.

"No holds barred, gentlemen." Loversall joined Trewithick.

No holds barred, hey? Dunkley knew, and they knew he knew, several things that would end the challenge in seconds.

I will not be my father. I am not a Black Dunkley.

However much the fool asked for it.

Dunkley set his stick on the ground and hooked a thumb on the waistband of his jogging pants, assuming a casual pose.

"Cast this plague from me." Still out of breath from the previous unexpected attack, he controlled his complaining lungs as he watched the other student's preparations. Every second ffalkenham delayed was an extra moment of recovery for him.

Normally, taking on any ten fellow apprentices—like ffalkenham's cheerleaders who arranged themselves against the wall to watch—wasn't a problem but Dunkley regretted the last half hour he had spent training with Marishes, the only student who gave him a decent match.

Marishes hooked a climbing rope over to where he hung from a climbing frame and eased himself, hand over hand, to the floor. He shoved a low beam balance bar over to the wall opposite ffalkenham's gang and flipped it over into a bench. Sagging down onto it he leaned back against the wall and closed his eyes. Dunkley wished joining his sparring partner for a rest was an option.

Moments later, ffalkenham charged. *"He ordaineth arrows against the persecutors."*

Dunkley raised his aching arms to chest height, holding the hiking stick horizontally. *"The Lord is my strength and my shield."*

ffalkenham's imaginary arrows hit the wall on either side. Using the words in the Book of Common Prayer, it was possible to imagine everything.

Dunkley swiped at ffalkenham's feet. ffalkenham jumped, but it broke his forward momentum just enough. Dunkley whipped his stick up and braced with both hands on his stick as ffalkenham shunted him against the bars, but without the weight from the charge.

Dunkley's hiking stick drank the impact; the prayers spread the force along the stick. The humming vibrations popped the rubber ferule off the end of the hiking stick, exposing the iron spike. The two men struggled face to face, with their sticks held between them. ffalkenham bore down on Dunkley with his greater height and weight

Not content with giving the upstart Scottish laird a thrashing, ffalkenham intended to harm or even kill. Would the tutors stop the fight? Maybe, maybe not.

"*And in the evening they will return to the city and grin like a dog,*" ffalkenham said.

Dunkley's exhausted muscles twitched as he resisted ffalkenham's desire to choke him with the oaken staff. "*Let me never be put to confusion.*"

ffalkenham insisted on tradition. Like everyone around here, he used the approved words and never innovated. These particular words were a traditional jape for use on first years.

Dunkley kicked up his knee; ffalkenham thrust his groin to one side, so Dunkley stamped down with his trainer on ffalkenham's instep. "*Thou smitest mine enemies on the cheekbone.*"

ffalkenham's chin jerked over his shoulder. With the leverage of his hiking stick, Dunkley shoved ffalkenham and surged away from the climbing frame.

"*He falleth down and...*" ffalkenham began

Dunkley stabbed at a hanging punch ball with his stick. The worn leather bag swung at ffalkenham's head, who ducked, and the ball thumped against the frame. Some Sassenachs only had one brain cell; distract them and they had to start again and you knew what to defend against.

"*He falleth down and humbleth himself.*" ffalkenham's voice echoed heroically among the roof beams.

"*I shall never be cast down. There shall be no harm happen unto me,*" Dunkley said.

The rebounding punch ball banged into ffalkenham's back, sending a squawk to join the echoes. He squirmed out of the way of the swinging ball. He stared at Dunkley, who stood unhurt.

"That's not possible." ffalkenham glanced at the tutors. "Is he using his black magic?"

"No," Werlow said. "Dunkley, stop playing with your food, boy."

Was Werlow telling him to use black magic? No! Dunkley would end this without resorting to foul methods.

"That's crap! He's not one of us." ffalkenham snapped down his oaken staff to aim at Dunkley. "*He cast forth lightnings and destroyed them.*"

"*I have kept me from the ways of the destroyer.*" Dunkley leaned on his hiking stick, to keep on his feet but he knew it appeared infuriately casual. He flicked a glance at Werlow, who rubbed his lips as the lightning fizzled, falling to the floor with a smell of melting wax polish.

Face twisted into an unholy grimace, ffalkenham rushed at Dunkley holding his stick high above his head—like a cane to thrash a peasant.

"*He hath graven and digged up a pit, and is fallen into the destruction that he made for another,*" Dunkley said.

ffalkenham sprawled on the floor. He rolled, and halted as he took in the spike of Dunkley's hiking stick at his throat.

ffalkenham glared back; sweat beaded on his forehead.

No one would stop him. Werlow and Loversall leaned against the wall with their arms folded. Marishes eyed him as if he were an odd creature in a zoo. Not even ffalkenham's cheerleading pack complained—though one of them glanced at the waiting tutors.

Dunkley stared down the length of his hiking stick. His arms quivered with both exhaustion and black rage. One thrust would end this nuisance forever. No more taunts about being a Dark Lord. No more reminders he was a 'Black Dunkley'. Maybe force would get him respect from these bloody Sassenachs.

From the corner of his eye, Dunkley saw Werlow flick a glance at Trewithick, who bit the edge of his thumb.

They all know I'm a black sorcerer.

"Go ahead, Dark Lord," ffalkenham hissed.

Arms shaking with rage, Dunkley forced his stick away and rested the spike on the floor. "If I were what you believe, I wouldn't hesitate. Get up. You make the floor untidy."

I am not my father. Dunkley stalked away.

Trewithick's mouth opened to shout as he raised a hand.

Dunkley pivoted, his stick pointing at where ffalkenham raced in pursuit. "*He shall not suffer thy foot to be moved.*"

ffalkenham became a fleshy statue of a running man. He tried to call out, but his mouth stuck fast.

Dunkley scooped up the rubber ferule—he'd have to re-work his method of dispersing force in order to keep the ferule in place—and left ffalkenham trapped. The tutors strode past him to inspect ffalkenham. Werlow nodded approval at Dunkley. ffalkenham's cheerleaders slunk out of the gymnasium.

At the door, Dunkley flipped over one of the low-beam bars and turned it into a bench. His hiking stick clattered against the wood as he threw it down. He stripped off his sweat-soaked tee shirt, dropping it next to the stick, and examined the bruises on the side of his rib cage.

Trewithick joined him. "Time to release ffalkenham."

"He'll drop into a puddle of his own piss." Dunkley prodded the gray patches on his arm where more bruises were forming. "*Oh Lord heal, me for my bones are vexed.*"

Trewithick leaned in, trapping him with a friendly arm against the wall. To all others in the room it would appear as if Trewithick congratulated his friend.

"So that's going to convince them you're not a sodding little Dark Lord, is it?"

Dunkley would only take the 'little' from Trewithick despite most of the collegiate topping six foot to his 5'10".

"Give it a rest, Trewithick; I can fight my own bullies now. What do you care for them?"

"I was the one who fought so hard to get you accepted at the college," Trewithick said

"Yes, we're good—"

Cold pricked Dunkley's chest. He glanced down; Trewithick held his silver-plated knife in the right place to slide through Dunkley's ribs to stop his heart. Dunkley watched Trewithick's face.

"And I'm the one who has to kill you if you are a black sorcerer," Trewithick said.

Dunkley held his breath. He would never raise a hand against Trewithick.

"So less of the arrogant Lairdling, and more Humble Servant of the Church, if you please." Trewithick barred his teeth in a fierce grin. He slid his knife away. Dunkley had no idea where his friend kept it.

"If nothing else," Trewithick continued. "The poor cleaners would have to re-wax the floor after mopping up the mess."

Brushing Trewithick's arm aside, Dunkley retrieved his stick and pointed it at ffalkenham. From their frowns, the two tutors were flummoxed by the immobility. Their confusion filled Dunkley with an—yes, he would admit it—arrogant pleasure.

"Gentlemen?" Dunkley had the tutors' full attention. "Stand aside, please."

A path opened to ffalkenham.

"Thank you." With his stick directed at his victim, in a loud, clear voice he said, "*Know this also, that the Lord hath chosen to himself the man that is godly; when I call upon the Lord, He will hear me.*"

ffalkenham staggered as the immobility ceased. Mr. Loversall caught him, but he stared at Dunkley.

Dunkley nodded; let the old fogies try and figure out how he did that one.

Storm Damage

The next wave crashed over the seafront pub. Water lashed the chimney pots and dislodged tiles. The wave raced up the neighboring river channel and smashed against the bridge, sending a wall of water over the men inspecting the span. It washed down the road and broke as a smaller wave against the front doors of the darkstone terrace of houses lining the road to the seafront.

Householders raced to build sandbag barriers over their front doors before the wind drove another wall of water into town on the high tide.

Trewithick gauged the speed of the incoming wave and leaned over the parapet to inspect the stonework.

"Sir Nathaniel!"

Trewithick dashed to the other side of the bridge, shielding his face from the stinging salt water. Pebbles battered his trench coat and along with his companions he ducked his head below his shoulders for the minimal protection it gave. Underfoot, the bridge shuddered and the stones ground against each other. Cracks ran the length of the tarmac. The pebbles and stones hurled by the waves created pothole-like craters in the road surface.

"Well?" the coast guard yelled over the wind.

"It's not going to hold the night with this storm," Trewithick shouted back.

"I told you it would take a miracle to have it hold," the coastguard said.

The harbor master squinted into the driven rain. "If it's this bad here, what it's like down towards the Lizard? Our headland protects Finnmouth."

Trewithick planted the spike of his hiking stick between two stones and clung on as the landing wave washed over the bridge. The harbor master grabbed for the wall as the whole structure shook.

"They're getting bigger," he screamed.

"It's the Morgawr churning up the sea out there," the coastguard shouted back.

Trewithick wiped over his glasses and squinted over the harbor wall. That would be one for his notebook if he spotted it. He saw nothing but another wall of water bearing down on the town. "You think so?"

"Sir Nathaniel! Don't you go teasing an old man by pretending to believe him. Sea serpents! What next?" The harbor master thumped the coastguard's shoulder. "You'll be hearing the bells from the drowned foreshore church of St Blaise."

Bugger. With his time at the college, he'd forgotten in this modern age no one believed Cryptozoology a legitimate subject for study. It was better that way, just inconvenient when you fought Creatures of the Night as your job.

Hooking the retaining strap of the hiking stick over his wrist, Trewithick let the wind blow him along the road. He drew the two older men with him into the relative shelter of an ice cream shop doorway. Even here the rain pelted against the men's waterproofs like a constant drumroll.

"Since you mention St Blaise, we don't want any more dead kiddies in our town. I've got Trewithick Hall opened up to evacuate people from the harbor front. Mrs. Penlerick found all the old blankets from when the Hall was commandeered as a school for World War Two evacuees. Someone thrifty stored them away properly, not a moth in sight. She was stacking them by the front door as I answered the phone."

The harbor master snorted. "We'd better get half the town up there or we'll never hear the end of how useless we all are."

The coastguard eyed the darkness out at sea. "I'll take the west foreshore if you knock on the doors for the east. What will you do, Sir Nathaniel?"

"Inspect the harbor wall, make sure it's holding," Trewithick said.

"You might want to check the river defenses too." The harbor master pointed up the hill. "The Parish Council intended to bring up the subject of the mill race. Some of the stone there is eroding away."

"I'll do that," Trewithick said.

The two older men braved the howling gale that drove the sea onto the land. Trewithick waited a moment longer in the relative shelter until they were no longer in view. He had another idea in mind and wanted the older men out of the way. He had sensed something in the bridge piers and the abutment when he had laid a hand on the parapet earlier and he wanted to know if it had been real or a storm-wrought hallucination.

He watched another towering wave crash over the bridge and then staggered out into the storm force winds. Bracing his staff in the stones again, he stripped off his gloves and laid a hand on the ancient stonework.

Water lashed his face and he ducked below the parapet into the negligible shelter it provided. He wiped his face and gasped out, *"His pavilion around him with dark water."*

The water stopped about an inch from his head and tumbled around him like a waterfall. Unless he was mistaken those waves were larger with every onslaught. He stood again and laid his hands on the stone—he needed his friend Carr who could read stones like they were a manuscript.

"For I have an eye unto all his laws."

He sensed it. Deep inside the stones of the bridge some ancestor of his had laid a working to strengthen the bridge against storms like this one. It overlaid an even earlier spell someone had worked into the river banks to support the predecessor of this bridge, built to replace the expensive ferry service or half a day's walk upstream to a ford.

The surging tide threw another wall of water at him. His protection stopped the soaking but the force in the wave drove him off the bridge. He retreated to the semi-sheltered doorway.

If he added more power to both the spells, this bridge might hold the night. Once he'd shored up the bridge he needed to check on the harbor wall and find out if his ancestor had also used illicit practical theology to strengthen that as well.

Many Trewithicks over the years had joined the Church as Witch-Finders—not all of them with the best intentions. He felt no surprise in discovering the working on the bridge, after all, he had considered the action himself—even with all the vows the College required of the Collegiate.

Strengthening what was already present was hardly a misuse of anything. He let a wave tumble over the bridge and dashed out. Laying his hands on the stone, he gathered his strength.

Out in the bay the surf roared. Thunder crashed against the headland; the flickering lightning illuminated the tempestuous sea.

And more.

There *was* a Morgawr out in the bay. He was sure of it. It roiled about, rocked by the waves—or rocking them, as the coastguard would have it. Strengthening the bridge came first then dealing with the sea serpent.

"*For thou shalt—*"

The creature roared. It seethed the bay and sent a ferocious wave racing towards the shore.

His protections wouldn't stand against that one. Trewithick raced back to the shelter of the doorway as the wave broke higher than the top of the seafront pub.

The house was three stories high, yet water tumbled over the roof into the road.

Trewithick braced against the doorposts as water rolled over the seafront houses and into the streets beyond. It washed as high as his waist. He pressed his hands and feet hard against the walls of his alcove as the water tugged at him, trying to drag him out to sea on the return.

Did the creature want to eat drowned Witch-Finder?

He had to steady the bridge. If it went down it would cut off the only road out of the town. It might be months before anyone rebuilt it.

No fish, no matter how big, was going to stop him from protecting his town. Most of the people here were his tenants. He braced again as another wave crashed over the seafront. When the water rolled away he bolted onto the bridge. More waves bore down on the small town but he planted the spike of his hiking stick in a crack as an extra post to cling to.

"*He shall lead me forth beside the waters of comfort.*"

Calm washed out over the water. The waves as they reached the shore only crashed halfway up the seafront pub.

The Morgawr howled, thrashing its coils in the bay.

Trewithick laid his hand over the parapet again. *"For thou shalt save the people who are in adversity."*

His working meshed with those already in place, feeding in power. This matched his opinion they were put in place by members of the Witch-Finder's College. The bank strengthened and the pillars of the bridge toughened.

Trewithick sank down below the parapet drained but happy he had saved his people, but he still needed to check the sea defenses.

Out in the bay the Morgawr keened an urgent lament. The coils still churned up the bay but it had lost their former intensity. Was it because it knew the bridge would hold? But why would that matter? Surely the creature had been creating mischief. The sea serpent's call echoed off the headland and around the bay until it sounded like more than one sea creature singing.

With the draining of his strength, the working calming the bay waters lost its power. As the Morgawr continued thrashing its coils the waves built up again.

There *were* two voices in the song. The higher pitched one sang on the landward side of the bridge. Heaving on the parapet he climbed to his feet and staggered over to the other side of the cracked and broken road. Wave after wave washed over him, but he stared into the waters below. Normally with all the run off from the hills in this storm the water would be racing to the bay, but the high tide pushed against the flow; the river was almost still.

Breaking the surface was a scrawny eel-like creature, singing along with the Morgawr in a thready voice speaking of illness and despair.

Trewithick stared at the creature, and it stared back. He glanced over his shoulder and watched the Morgawr send more waves crashing down on the town. Then he looked back at the silvery eel.

It was a radical idea, but was this the Morgawr's offspring? Did a Morgawr head up river to spawn like salmon? Had the smolt been trapped? He leaned on the bridge parapet and studied the creature. Nothing blocked the span beneath the bridge so the bridge itself must be the obstacle. That meant the Morgawr had spawned in 17-something or other—he'd have to check the exact date the bridge had been built. What was the lifecycle of these creatures? He had found nothing in the College's library.

The voice of the eel under the bridge faded. Trewithick saw it was weak. It was large for an eel; the river would not hold enough food; was the Morgawr smolt starving to death?

Trewithick stared into the darkness. Along the main street of the town he heard new noises. Cars ran up the hill to the Hall, taking the families from the seafront to safety. Of course the bridge would block the smolt: it was a Creature of the Night and opposing magic was laid down on the bridge. And he had increased the repulsion by adding to the spell.

He glanced down; the creature below him stopped its song. From the way the Morgawr thrashed, it was building up to destroy the town in punishment for the death of its child.

He had to do something or the whole town would be washed into the sea along with the church from—oh yes, the church full of children sheltering from a storm like this one had been washed into the sea the year the bridge had been built. No connection had been made, but Trewithick saw it now. The smolt must have tried to join its parent and the Morgawr had killed the children when its own child was trapped.

Removing his strengthening would destroy the bridge leaving the town cut off for months while a new one was built. He could fight the Morgawr in the bay. Or…?

What were his options here?

He considered the flood defenses along the river. Where was the weakest point? Something in the minutes of the parish council meeting, oh yes. The stone in the mill race was weakening. With the high tide backing up the river, if that gave way the town would be flooded.

Which was better? Trying to fight the Morgawr out on the harbor wall or letting a flood race through town to let the Morgawr smolt out to sea. The eel-like creature lifted its head in another song to its parent out in the bay. The sound was feebler now.

He was already weak from shoring up the bridge defenses he doubted he would win a fight with the creature out in the bay. So that left flooding the town.

He'd better not let anyone catch him trashing the mill race.

"He made darkness his secret place," he whispered. The roar of the fierce storm drowned out his words, but the working settled into place.

Cars rushed up through the town. The rain already transformed the street into a river. He waded up the main street, ducking into shadows as cars full of refugees raced up the hill. Waves washed the street, sometimes the cars floated back towards the shore front until the water drained away and tires touched down on tarmac.

His town was going to slide into the sea.

He waded against the flow of the water and headed down a side street. Here no one was evacuating, but unless he released the Morgawr smolt this whole town was doomed. Not even the Hall would survive the onslaught should the Morgawr's offspring perish. Against that, a little flood was a problem easily mopped up.

The river clawed at the walls of the mill race. Squinting in the dark he examined the race until he found the portion of concern to the parish council. The mortar holding the stones had perished, only force of habit kept the stones in place, in fact it might not even need his help to fail.

First he had to summon the smolt. *"But they are all gone out of the way, they are altogether become abominable."*

The Morgawr in the bay howled its despair and rage at his action. It would assume he was about to destroy its child. The rage washed over the town in the form of more waves. The cars, which carried people to refuge, had all passed.

He was alone in the storm-wracked streets.

On the seafront a house collapsed in a thundering crash, but he held to the summoning.

The silvery eel fluttered through the water. It had no strength to resist his call. It lay still in the water that lapped to his feet.

He stuck his hiking stick into the mill race wall and pushed against the loosely held stonework.

He glanced at the houses around him. Lights were on, but no one called to stop him from his vandalism: his hiding spell must be working.

The smolt watched him. The first stone fell into the water. The smolt darted away in alarm but came back to watch as he worked at the second stone.

It thrashed its coils in imitation of the adult Morgawr in the bay. The extra aggravation of the water undermined the stone and it fell into the water. The smolt continued its thrashing.

Yes, it was going to get free. The huge volumes of water held back by this wall trickled through the abused stonework.

He ran.

Behind him stone crashed as the wall gave way. An express train of water chased him down the road. Screams rang out from householders as water flooded through their front doors.

The leading edge lapped around his feet. "*Let not the water-flood drown me.*"

His feet splashed down in knee deep water as he angled to the higher ground on the bridge. Another wave smashed into the shore and crashed over the bridge.

Trewithick clutched onto the stone parapet as water from everywhere tugged and smashed into him.

His glasses washed away in the flood blurring everything, but riding on the crest of the flood wave through town he saw the silvery Morgawr smolt. As it reached the sea it sang to the larger Morgawr.

The Creature in the bay calmed. The waves dropped to half their former size, normal for a wind-driven storm.

Trewithick crawled up the bridge until he was higher than the flood racing through town. The waves ceased trying to wash him off the bridge. He huddled down, too drained even to summon enough heat to ward off the chilling wind.

Through the storm he heard the songs of the two Morgawr in the bay.

Private Security

A picturesque town was not the sort of place you'd expect trouble, beyond the odd rowdy youth. Simeon Carr parked by the river so he could walk through the market square and get a feel for the place before he started work.

A young man wearing vicar blacks and dog collar thwarted this desire. He ran over, his cheeks glowing in enthusiasm. Carr lifted the rear door on the hatchback and his Border Collie sprang out. He sniffed at the tarmac then followed a trail of something to the grass, tail wagging in a blur. Jesse always brought a smile to Carr's face. The best dog he'd ever trained. He lifted out his bag of tools and locked the car—some days the tools weighed more than others. Today in the bright sunlight it was easy to carry.

The young vicar hitched aside his jacket and produced a small notebook from his back pocket. "I've taken notes, sir. It always happens when a family with a dog rents Back Barrough House for their holiday."

Carr glanced up and down the quiet high street. "Show me which house, please. That'll do!" The Border Collie, which had been sniffing at a lamppost, returned to heel.

The vicar jerked his head at the odd exclamation at the end of the sentence and noticing the dog's obedience he decided it wasn't for him. "It's this way, Mr. Carr."

Carr fell in beside Powell as the vicar led the way into town. Jesse trotted alongside.

"Tell me more about this 'phantom dog' of yours, Mr. Powell."

"It appears during thunderstorms, but has been witnessed at other times." Powell read from his notes. "Wherever it goes, it leaves scorch marks on the brickwork. It set fire to the local bus shelter; the council replaced it with that metal monstrosity. There were loud questions about the activities of local youths, but those have died down again. The owners of the house are absent, an old local family but these days they live in Spain. The townsfolk have made the same connection I did: Back Barrough House and dogs. 'Mr. Powell' they told me. 'You've got to do an exorcism or sommat'." He mimicked the local accent. "I thought I'd better call in the experts."

"And it's not killed anyone?" Carr strolled along behind the local vicar, taking in the whole market town.

"Not that I know of," Powell said. "It emerges with its glowing red eyes and 'riding' on lightning—that's what the witnesses say."

"You are not one of the witnesses?"

"I live on the other side of town, in the new estate. No one has seen it over there." He stopped in front of an old half-timbered house. "And here it is, Mr. Carr."

The house stood on the main street through the small town. A cobbled alley ran next between it and the shop next along. A sign fixed to the shop wall declared it to be Copse Lane.

Carr studied the old building Powell indicated was at the center of the problem. It resembled every other half-timbered house in every tourist trap in the country. Except for one thing: on the front corner next to the alleyway it had a corner stone, a pillar that ran halfway up the side of the building—the rest of the house was constructed in brick and plaster.

Carr crouched down and opened his bag. "Make sure no one is watching too closely." He waited until Powell had checked the street. He stripped off his leather driving gloves and dropped them in the open mouth of his bag.

"Jesse! There!" The Collie lay beside the open bag, head up on alert.

This task was going to require flesh to stone.

From a little pocket set into his bag, he pulled out a little bottle of rosemary essential oil. He rubbed a drop on his temples and onto the palms of his hands. Memories tugged at him before he even recapped the bottle. Now, he needed clear sight.

He laid his oiled palms on the stone pillar. "*Surely thou hast seen it, for thou beholdest ungodliness and wrong.*"

People sang in low minor tones as they trod the road marked out by planks laid over the boggy ground. They carried a body between the pillars and onwards towards the only high ground. Around them the ancestors gathered ready to welcome the newly dead into their ranks.

"Corpse way not copse way," Carr muttered. "Nothing to do with trees."

"I beg your pardon?" Powell hesitated a moment. "What are you doing?"

Carr lifted his head, blinking to try and refocus on today. "Each man at the College is gifted with some special ability which helps us in our work. I can read the memories from stone." Grief of the mourners rolled over him. "Is there an old Barrow around here?" He studied the alleyway beside the house. "Perhaps down here?"

"Copse Lane? That leads to the Church—by the back door so to speak. It leads to the oldest part of the graveyard. If you ask me, that's why the owners live in Spain and let out the cottage to holiday makers."

It made sense. "Do you have the key to the house? Or must I perform a break and entry? The College prefers we use keys to crowbars."

Powell searched his jacket pockets and held out a key ring. "I picked them up from the letting agency before you arrived. The agent's a local man, he understands."

"Thank you." Carr accepted the two keys and waved a rosemary scented hand at the alleyway. "This is liminal space."

"Huh?"

Carr fitted one of the keys into the lock. "Not this one… typical. A liminal space is one where the veil between this world and the next is thin. Black dogs are known to guard such transitional spaces; this is the type of creature you have described. Was the town gallows located near here?"

Powell's mouth dropped open and he pointed across the road at where a similar alleyway vanished between two warehouses. "It was over there."

Carr noted the proximity of the two alleys to the main road. "A crossroads, of course," he murmured. "What did you call this house?" With effort he focused on Powell. Images of carts carrying plague dead filled his head. It wasn't even a large town but they had suffered greatly and Carr suffered with them.

"Back Barrough House."

"Etymology. Time has change Corpse Lane to Copse Lane. Barrough is where barrow ended up, so this would be the house at the back of the barrow. That's higher ground over there. I suspect your churchyard contains a pre-historic barrow burial ground."

Powell grimaced. "I suppose we do tend to build on the old Pagan sites, to sanctify and purify them."

Purifying fires burned night and day at the barrow. Old carved gods and roman statues thrown on as the villagers dared not speak out. The ancestors stood behind the living, but they faded.

Carr's hands curled up into a fist; he controlled an urge to punch that fresh shining face. He spun to face the young vicar. Powell must be almost straight from the seminary in his first post. In this day and age a young man as a vicar was almost an oddity, most had live full other lives before being called to serve God.

"All things are sacred," Carr hissed.

Powell stepped back. He stumbled over an uneven paving slab, but kept his horrified eyes on Carr. "Yes, of course, Sir."

Carr closed his eyes and counted to ten. He'd been losing his temper too often. He released the anger at Powell's ill-thought-out comment. "Yes, quite." He cleared his throat and opened the door to cover his confusion. "You mentioned the effect manifested when a dog entered the house?"

"That's correct."

Carr returned to his bag. He unstrapped a slim wand of rowan wood. "That'll do." The dog stood and trotted at his master's side. "Powell, stay here for now. I'm not sure what will happen, best if you're somewhere without a roof to fall on you, hey?"

Powell scrambled away from the house. He stood by the edge of the road as Carr went inside and closed the door.

"*Forsake me not, O Lord, be thou not far from my side.*" He awakened the prayers of protection in his wand that he had imbued in the wood over his many years of practice. Clutching it in his left hand, the hand of the heart, he opened the door

As he stepped onto the polished-wood floor, whispered memories drifted into his mind without touching his ears. This house overflowed with people who had lived their whole lives here. From the more recent past, holiday makers flitted through in instant. They left minimal impression: sorrows and deep anger were more likely to leave a mark for him to sense.

A wall patched from where a drunken husband missed when his wife ducked. His pain and resentment—how dare she dodge her just punishment—filled this part of the corridor. With on hand on Jesse's head, Carr went where he was led. He had no sense of his feet and relied on the Collie to keep him in touch with now.

The daughter of the house and a footman coupled, each listening for a footstep that would show them betrayed to the master of the house.

A thousand screaming, resentful first breaths, myriad slides into the last light, a couple of dozen violent ends—pleas for mercy painted onto the lath and plaster walls crowded into his head.

He compartmented these memories away from his real memories, so when he had sorted out which were important here he could forget them all later. Without the ability to forget the other people's pain and pleasure he would go mad.

Fear and pain: so long ago this house was little better than a one-room dwelling. A scrabbling at the walls and whining.

A noise in his ears called him back to the present. Jesse choked and hacked.

"O spare me a little, that I might recover my strength."

Carr dropped to his knees on the flags the paved this small room—it held a washing machine and tumble dryer with pegs for wet weather gear. An old towel hung next to a sink. He ran a hand over Jesse's back.

"What is it, boy?"

His dog vomited over the floor, and backed out of the room. At the door, Jesse set his feet with raised hackles and growled at the wall opposite.

Carr slid from his knees to a wary crouch. He slowly stood, keeping his eyes on the wall and his rowan wand ready. First one step then another as he backed away from the wall nearest the pile of dog vomit. The stench of recycled dog food mixed with the colder scent of washing powder.

The hand holding the rowan wood wand touched a window sill and, dragging his knuckles on the plaster, he slid along the outer wall. A quick glance outside showed him Powell remained, shifting from foot to foot on the edge of the path.

This room must be the one with the ancient pillar set into the corner, but plaster covered the evidence in here.

Thunder boomed and the room shuddered. The vibrations shattered the old plaster like a dropped mirror. Black tar oozed out of cracks. It dripped down the lime-washed wall like tears of old blood.

Balanced on his toes, Carr held the wand in front of him, at chin height, waiting to decide on action. Jesse's growls intensified; his tail down and stiff.

The scent of rosemary drifted to Carr's nose from where it coated his palms

Whining in the dark. Frantic scratching, growing more feeble now.

The tar shadow formed into a child's crayon drawing on the wall: a sharp face, four legs under a brick of a body and a raggedy tail. Then the picture pushed away from the wall. The first leg touched the stone flags of the floor and crackled with electricity.

Jesse crouched in challenge as the second foot burst free of the wall.

"Get out! Get back!" Carr ordered.

Jesse fled with his tail between his legs as the memories flooded over Carr.

With banging drums and loud squawking brass trumpets, the people led the cowering dog to the wall of the new house. The noises would scare away all the demons—they terrified the small dog. The sacrifice would provide a guardian for as long the family lived here. With ceremony, the dog was lifted into the gap and the last bricks were put in place, locking the dog in a dark place.

At first the dog slept because it was dark. Then it got hungry and thirsty. It howled out its distress and scratched the wall to get out. Finally it whined while it lay in the dark. Why had they left it alone?

Then there was only the dark and silence—for eternity.

Carr wrenched his mind away from the memories. He had to be here and now. The shadow dog now had three legs away from the wall. Only one back leg and the tail were still a child's scribble on the whitewashed wall.

He shifted his grasp on the rowan. The demon dog's glowing red eyes followed the stick.

Carr stepped back, but the dog's eyes stayed on the wand. Its last leg free came free and it bounded forward, yanking the tail out of the plaster. It was still a smudge in the air as if it was coal smoke, but it was recognizably a dog.

It stretched back leaning on its elbows, eyes fixed on the wand. What?

The tail wagged with cracks of the lightning like whips. The dog growled menacingly but that tail wagged.

Carr waggled the wand. "You want to play, boy?"

The dog jumped up running in a circle. It barked like thunder and wagged its tail. Then it returned to the crouched growl.

Carr waggled the wand in front of the dog's nose. It pounced on the wand and began a tug of war.

Laughing, Carr hauled back. Even using two hands the dog nearly had him over. The flagstones under foot cracked at the heat of the lightning sparking off the excited dog. Carr was grateful for the thick soles on his boots; normally they prevented any of his workings from grounding out. This time they stopped him from being electrocuted by a lightning dog.

He switched tactics and pulled the wand sideways out of the dog's mouth.

He held the wand above his head. "Want to play fetch? Come on, boy!" No, that was wrong. "Come on, Lightning!"

The dog bounced all around him, trying to reach the stick and growling in mock menace. Carr backed out of the room. The lightning dog followed him. Sparks melted the varnish on the polished wood floor in the hall into the form of paw prints.

"Come on, Lightning! Come play fetch!" He led the dog out of the house onto the street.

Powell stared at him then at the smoky image of the dog. Jesse edged forward to sniff at the new dog's tail. He sneezed as a spark hit his nose.

"Here, Lightning! Fetch!" Carr lobbed the wand down the street.

The smoky dog charged after it.

Carr admired the running dog with its tail wagging joyfully at the game. What could he do with a dog like this? Train it like Jesse and … no. His heart sank. He loved the smoky dog already but it was a dangerous creature that would kill from exuberance. He clenched his fists.

Powell sidled closer. "It wants to play?"

Carr nodded unable to speak as Lightning sprinted back and dropped the wand at his feet. The spirit dog backed away, circling and barking, tail pounding the air. Sparks of lightning flew everywhere.

Carr crouched. Keeping his boots as the contact with the pavement, he scratched Lightning behind the ears. It was like tickling solid air. It was ice cold and burning hot at the same moment.

"Good dog! You want to play? Stay back, Powell." In his peripheral vision he saw as Powell, who had been inching forward to join the playful dog, skittered away.

Carr surged up with the wand in his hand. He waved it about to tease the playful pup. Then he lobbed it down Copse Lane. The dog hurled itself after the stick in a crescendo of barks.

Still watching Lightning, he said, "Powell, in my bag you'll find a hammer. Take it and smash the wall in the room there, above where Jesse vomited. Bring me what you find."

Lightning charged back, carrying the now burning rowan wand. It dropped the stick at Carr's feet.

"Good dog!" Carr stamped out the flames. He played more tug of war with Lightning as he heard pounding on the wall inside the utility room.

"Good dog! Good, Lightning." The dog nearly tugged him off his feet. The pounding stopped and he saw Powell emerge from the house carrying a small bundle.

"Here! Lightning! Get the Stick! Fetch!" Again he hurled the stick up Copse Lane, Lightning's smoky claws clattered on the cobbles as he raced away.

Powell walked across the pavement and handed the small dog skeleton wrapped in a towel to Carr.

"It's a puppy," Powell whispered. "It was walled up in there."

"It was walled up alive. In most places this would have caused no problems, except for cruelty to the dog. Because this is a liminal space, the death terror of the puppy called a nature spirit."

He took the bones and laid them out in order on the pavement. Lightning ran back. It dropped the burning wand and sniffed at the bones.

"I've brought you out of the darkness, Lightning. You'll never be in the dark again."

Lightning nosed at the bones.

"It's time for a nap. *They are even as sleep and fade away suddenly.*" Carr spread his hands over the pitiful bones as Lightning circled them. It settled in a curled ball around the bones. The smoky dog-form sank into the skeleton.

"*Our days are gone and our years of toil at an end.*" Carr held out his hand to Powell. "My hammer."

Powell placed the lump hammer onto his outstretched palm.

"But it's tamed! You don't need to destroy—"

"The spirit went mad when the family it was supposed to protect left it alone." Carr kept his voice level. "It tries to drive away the intruders in the house, waiting for the family to return."

He crouched, holding the hammer over the skeleton. Closing his eyes against the tears, he let the hammer fall.

Jesse howled in anguish from where he lay by the bag of tools. Carr pounded the bones into crumbs, and then with the hammer head he ground them into dust. He gathered them up into his hands. Head still bowed over he held them out to the local vicar.

Reluctantly, Powell offered cupped hands and Carr poured in the powdered remains of Lightning.

"Take them and scatter them on the river with proper prayers for the dead. I promised him … I promised no more being walled away in the dark."

"Couldn't you have—?"

"Do it!" Carr dropped his hammer into the bag. It thunked heavily. Collecting the charred remains of his rowan wand, he set this inside the bag as well. Carr picked up his bag of tools: it dragged at his arm as if it weighed a ton.

"Your job is so hard." Tears leaked down Powell's cheeks. With his hands cradling the remains of the puppy, he trotted down to the river.

Carr watched Powell all the way to the river. With his free hand, Carr retrieved his mobile phone and dialed a number he knew by heart.

It answered at once.

"I'm sorry." The tears falling for Lightning cracked his voice. "I can't do this job anymore."

Putting the phone away, Carr walked after Powell to the riverside car park.

"That'll do!"

Jesse climbed to his feet and followed his master.

The Loathly Bride

Simeon tapped on the hotel room door, rattling his keys against the velvet covered box in his pocket as he waited. He heard the bolt drawn back.

"Jane, don't open all the way …" He wanted to let her know he was out here. She had superstitions.

A face appeared around the door, and it wasn't Jane. He had no idea Penny even knew her mother was getting married today.

She came out a little further. He wouldn't have matched that heavy pendant necklace with the floaty dress she wore, but young people had different fashions.

"Hi Simeon," Penny said. "You can't come in, you know. Groom can't see Bride before reaching the altar."

"Please ask Jane if she would do me the favor of sticking her hand around the door?"

Penny retracted her head but left the door ajar. "Mum, it's your boyfriend … oh sorry, fiancé."

Penny poked her head out again. "She's coming."

"What do you need, Simeon?" Jane sounded like she was on the other side of the door. "I'm not coming out while you're there."

"I want your hand."

"Well, you made that clear." Jane laughed. Penny sighed at the bad joke.

A hand snaked around between Penny and the door.

"The other one, please," Simeon said. "I need your left hand."

"Stop being so mysterious." Jane exchanged hands.

Simeon slipped the ring box out of his pocket. Penny gasped as he opened it and slipped a sapphire ring with an Art Deco lozenge setting onto Jane's ring finger.

Jane jerked her hand inside the door. "Simeon!"

"I hope you like it. I mean … if you don't mind second hand. Family tradition and all, but I can get a modern one if you—"

"It's fantastic!" She sounded stunned, but in a good way.

Simeon settled his shoulders to ease the tension. No matter how well he thought he knew her, there was always doubt. "It was my grandmother's. M'brother, Torquil, brought it up with him last night. It's a bit loose, but we can sort that out later."

"I would kiss you, but …"

"Later," Penny said. "Mind you Mum, you're missing a sight here. Simeon is … dapper—that's the word for a man of his generation." On that snarky remark, she closed the door and slid the bolt across again.

Simeon gazed at the closed door; in a little over an hour he and Jane would be together forever so the door was less of annoyance than it might be. Penny, however, needed more consideration. Even though he was retired from the Church Office, he kept his ear to the ground. He'd learned things about Miss Penny that were never going to reach her mother's hearing if Simeon had any say.

With his hands in the pockets of his sharply-creased, pin-striped trousers, he trotted down the stairs, the tails of his formal jacket flipping out behind him. There was something about that black glass pendant … later, he more important matters to attend today.

Torquil waited for him in the hotel lobby. God! but his brother was vain. Although he was older, Torquil had less gray in his hair than Simeon, except at his temples because that made him distinguished. Simeon grinned affectionately. While waiting for his brother, Torquil inspected the set of his cravat in a small hand mirror.

"Well, did she like it?" Torquil demanded, sliding the mirror into the pocket of his waistcoat. He wore similar morning clothes to Simeon, but whereas Simeon's cravat and double-breasted waistcoat were dove-gray, Torquil had gone for dusky pink. As Simeon strolled up to him, Torquil reached out and straightened the camellia in his brother's button hole.

"How could I tell? All I saw was a hand," Simeon said.

"Honestly Sim, you're as provoking as ever," Torquil said. "David is waiting with the car. We can go to church early and nervously pace the aisle."

Simeon tucked his hand through Torquil's arm. "You're acting as if you've never been to a wedding before. I see your David isn't on one of his unfaithful binges. I don't know how you put up with him: the Boomerang Lover."

Torquil squeezed his brother's arm. "Because he loves me really."

"You deserve better."

"Do you know, I've never met anyone other than you who is so alive. And despite our father's harsh words, I never would 'corrupt the morals' of my little brother."

They picked up their top hats from the table by the entrance to the hotel and stepped out into a cloud-covered day. Not bad for October, at least it wasn't raining—yet.

"We'd better stop by your house for some umbrellas," David Marishes said, as they emerged. He too was dressed in formal wear from a premium London tailor, though he favored a black waistcoat with his tasteful green cravat.

Despite Marishes's detour they arrived at the church with plenty of time before the wedding. Somewhere the back corner of the churchyard under its over-grown yew trees, an Anglo-Saxon king was rumored to be buried under a hog back gravestone, but the brambles and wild roses discouraged even the bravest local historian from searching him out.

Marishes wasn't the only old colleague present at the wedding. He must have mentioned the occasion to Dunkley.

Torquil elbowed Simeon as they walked through the stone lych-gate. "You've got the full 'Laird Alasdair' get up in honor of today."

It wasn't often Alasdair Dunkley wore the formal but startling Dunkley tartan, a kilt paired with a Bonnie Prince Charlie jacket and waistcoat. He knelt to pour water into a bowl for his dogs, settling them outside the Church porch. In deference to the threatening weather, he carried an Inverness cape.

Dunkley stood, folding the cape over his arm. He nodded to Marishes with an amused side-ways glance at Torquil. He held out his hand to Simeon.

"Congratulations, Carr," Dunkley said. "I hope you don't mind me dropping by. Trewithick's here as well."

"I saw him sidling around the back of the church for a crafty smoke." Simeon accepted the handshake. "Good of you to come. The wedding was never intended as a secret or anything, just quiet."

"I'm glad things have worked out between you and Jane, after this time and ..." Dunkley faded out, groping for a polite word.

"Yes, after what we did. Well, let's hope." Simeon glanced at the road and back towards the hotel. He surreptitiously checked his watch; there was still time for Jane to change her mind. Not that he thought she would, but ...

Dunkley held out a hand to greet Torquil, who responded with a hearty, "Laird Alasdair! Sooo good to see you."

Simeon batted at his brother for the camp byplay, and then wandered into the church. He set his top hat on the table near the door and walked towards the vestry to settle with the vicar. They had not arranged for flowers, this wasn't a big wedding, and the church smelled of cold candles, old incense and furniture polish.

Dunkley followed Simeon in and propped his hiking stick by the front door. He hung his cape on the coat stand, covering Trewithick's sword cane.

"Carr?" Dunkley's whisky gravel voice rumbled in the church roof vaulting.

Dunkley strode up the aisle between the two Churchwarden's Staves set into brackets on the last row of pews. His kilt swished around his knees and he'd dignified the occasion by wearing his short sword on his belt.

"I know it's not the best time," Dunkley said. "But we may not meet again for a while; you know how the job is."

Simeon leaned against wooden roses and ivy carved into a pew end. "Go on."

"As you're about to become Penny Bailey's step-father, would you teach her? She's bitter about exclusion from our training and you always were one of the better teachers."

Simeon raised his eyebrows. Church Inspectors did not under any circumstances teach women—the excuse used was they hadn't the stamina to use inherent cræft.

Dunkley grimaced. "I know, but it's tedious being required to house the female relatives of our Brothers at the Recovery Centre in Cambridge. Penny has a brother and a cousin in our College."

"Penny was helping her mother this morning. I'm not sure from her behavior she will respect anything I can say, but I'd already decided to try. It's nice to have official sanction."

"Semi-official, I'm afraid."

"Close enough for government work, hey?" Simeon said.

Marishes's querulous voice echoed through from the porch. "Do you have to be so outrageous when my colleagues are present, Tor?"

Simeon heard his brother's throaty chuckle, but didn't hear what he whispered in Marishes's ear as they entered the church. Marishes flushed as he set his topper on the table by the door.

Simeon leaned towards Dunkley and lowered his voice. "I expect you want me to keep the tuition a secret from Marishes?"

Dunkley scratched his short-cropped beard. "Probably best."

The conversation became general as Marishes and Torquil joined them and Simeon checked his pocket watch. Ten more minutes before Jane arrived. He'd waited eight years while she was in prison, so why was ten more minutes like torture?

Torquil smiled at him and reached over to straighten his cravat, yet again. "It will all be fine, Sim."

An almighty squealing emerged from the bowels of the church. Simeon dashed for the altar but the noise came from the side. The vicar dragged a table from the vestry. On it was laid the marriage register with an old-fashioned stylus pen and inkwell. Simeon stepped over to help him.

"I've been doing this for years," the vicar said. "Don't mess up your finery."

"Gives me something to do," Simeon said. "I'm twitchy."

The vicar checked his own watch. "She should be here shortly. I don't say five minutes because ladies on their wedding day need to get every detail right—"

A painful scream sounded in the churchyard, drowned out by a roar. Dunkley sprinted away. Within moments, he pulled open the door. Marishes paused only to grab both the churchwardens' staves from their brackets. He followed as Dunkley snatched up his hiking stick and Trewithick's sword cane.

Ice crept over Simeon's stomach. Something had happened to Jane.

Penny staggered into the church, her hands against her face. "There's a dragon!" Her voice was squeaky. "It's eaten Mum!"

"Jane!" Simeon couldn't move.

Dunkley pushed Penny aside and raced out of the church.

Marishes glanced over his shoulder at where Torquil stood near the empty brackets for the church warden's staves. His mouth dropped open as Marishes shed his prissy dancing teacher posture and become a fully armed Church Warrior.

"Stay with the girl, Tor." Marishes vanished after Dunkley.

Torquil rushed to Penny and wrapped an arm around the girl, leading her away from the door as the heavy oak swung shut. She sobbed into his shoulder.

For someone who had fled a dragon, her dress was pristine. *Consider that later*. Simeon darted glances around. He needed a wand. He hadn't come to Church prepared, like the others had. His eyes fixed on the registry stylus pen. He snatched it up: at least it had sanctity by virtue of its use in church.

The vicar grabbed at his arm. "The other men will rescue your lady from the dragon."

"Not if it's eaten her." He shook off the vicar's hand. He was going to slaughter the dragon. He would butcher it while it still lived.

Why had this happened now?

Simeon's best brogues pounded on the tiles of the aisle and echoed around the church. He reached the church doors and heaved on the handle. Behind him he heard Penny's sobs fading away and the vicar's footsteps as he trotted down the aisle to offer comfort.

Moving the heavy oak door was an effort, but he hauled it open. Outside the gray clouds had darkened even more. It was more like twilight than midmorning. He stepped out into the churchyard.

Beyond the church lych-gate, the limousine stood; the driver leaned on the car. If the man was watching maybe it wasn't as bad as Penny described. Most ordinary people would be a gibbering wreck at the appearance of a dragon.

Lying inside the church yard was some tattered pale blue fabric. The blue touched him and his eyes pricked with tears—so tactful, this wasn't Jane's first wedding, and Simeon had been instrumental in the death of her previous husband. Well, not able to prevent it, almost the same thing.

No blood. Simeon filed that fact away.

Marishes called out, answered by Trewithick: distance stole the words. The shouts came from round the side of the church. Simeon ran towards them. Rounding the buttress, he saw that even without his walking stick Trewithick had driven the hideous creature under a yew tree. Its skin reminded Simeon of a leprous toad and when it opened it mouth a decaying gas drifted out. The low branches prevented the beast from taking flight with its tattered and moldy wings.

Dunkley tossed the walking stick to Trewithick. Taking over the binding, Marishes braced the two staves on the ground and called out in a deep voice, so far from his usual querulous speech as to almost be from another person.

"They shall lay snares."

With its leg caught by invisible tethers, the dragon battered its wings against the low branches and unsightly gray-green feathers broke away from its pinions. Marishes held it down.

Simeon took a half-step back and averted his eyes from the creature. He held up a hand to block out the sight of the foul wyrm. This creature was more repulsive than normal. Perhaps because it had destroyed his happiness.

Dunkley and Trewithick unsheathed their swords. The pale autumn day filled with the song of the Universe. They spread out, one to each side and cosmic music of heaven surrounded them. Their sense of purpose calmed Simeon.

Simeon knew his role in this. Hadn't he been one of the Cardinal Angels, the Inner Circle, with these three men, before his retirement? Despite his desire to tear the dragon to shreds and stomp on it, his role was decoy—it always had been.

The dragon cawed in hoarse pain and sneezed its fire at Marishes. He crossed the staves in front of him.

"The voice of the Lord divides the flames."

The flames split to either side of Marishes. Behind him, Simeon heard a squeak of suppressed fear. Glancing back, he saw Torquil watching Marishes. His hands gripping the corner of the church were white.

The flames goaded Simeon into action. This dragon was weak of its kind, but still strong enough to take out a man, or woman. Holding the stylus he had picked up in church, he ran in front of Marishes. The flame died away, as if Simeon's action surprised the creature.

"Water the ground with my tears!" he shouted, lifting his hands to the clouded sky.

The lowering clouds let down a calculated gentle soaking rain—
a downpour would interfere with the fighters, a drizzle would be no
use at all. A chill fell with the rain, but the dragon steamed as it
hunched under the minimal shelter of the yew tree.

"Ross! Rory!" Dunkley shouted.

Dunkley's dogs raced around from where they had settled.
Barking, they harried the dragon's tail.

It twisted its body to move the tail away from its tormentors,
cracking the branches as it writhed in the limited space under the
branches. Angling its head this way and that to bring the dogs into
frame it snarled at them.

They danced out of the way. Dunkley's surprisingly bright kilt
flashed among the trees betraying his position as he tried creeping
into place.

The dragon aimed for the vivid movement, but the dogs gnawed
at the tail. Distracted by the dogs the dragon jerked back a leg,
trying to kick them off.

Holding his topper in place against the strong wind caused by
the thrashing wings, Trewithick circled around to the dragon's right
side.

Marishes's staves clattered on a grave stone. "*Not even the birds
can fly without your blessing,*" Marishes shouted.

The dragon slammed into the ground, flattened by Marishes's
words.

With the rain dripping in a constant shield against the fiery
exhalation, Simeon lowered his impromptu wand from the clouds.
He pointed it towards the dragon.

The dragon that had eaten Jane.

Trewithick and Dunkley were in place. The dogs worried at the
dragon's tail and it uttered one of its raucous cawing calls. It was the
most loathsome creature Simeon had ever encountered. It clawed at
the ground with its left talons, struggling to break Marishes's
working and flee.

"*Break thou the power of the ungodly!*" Simeon shouted.

The makeshift wand shattered in his hands. A spell had broken
somewhere, but Simeon was unable to identify what. The dragon
remained pinned to the ground. The gray-green feathers appeared
less moldy and more like moorland heather in winter. The leprous

quality of the scales faded. It called out again as it clawed the ground with its left claw; the harsh note had softened. It pleaded with him.

Simeon stared at it. At either side of the dragon, Dunkley's and Trewithick's swords had grown into great swords. Simeon had seen the transformation many times. Each time before, it had awed him. This time the dragon's eyes held his gaze.

The talons snagged in roots as the dragon clawed among the leaves shed by the brambles. Dunkley and Trewithick raised their great swords ready to finish the beast.

Then Simeon saw the claw.

The third claw on the left paw was twisted by a warped ring—a sapphire set into an Art Deco lozenge.

Stare into the dragon's eyes and your illusions are stripped away. You see the truth.

The dress had been unblooded.

"HOLD!" Simeon shouted.

Dunkley and Trewithick stood like statues, their swords raised over their heads. Simeon walked forward, his heart pulsing in his throat. If he were wrong, it would be his last mistake.

He knelt on a tombstone set into the earth. The cold stone chilled his knees even through the fine woolen fabric of his formal trousers. He lifted the twisted paw. The dragon wore his grandmother's ring.

"Jane? Are you in there?" he whispered.

It clawed again, sending rotting leaves flying and ripping out yew roots. The twisted arm stretched out. The claw with the ring on almost metamorphosed into being a finger, and then lurched back into talon form.

Dunkley lowered his weapon—it shrank back to a short sword. On the other side, Trewithick sheathed his sword into the Malacca cane. Behind them, Marishes kept the dragon pinned to the ground.

Simeon clenched his hand around the claw. "*My dove in the clefts of the rock, show me your face, let me hear your voice; for your voice is sweet and your face is lovely.*"

Gently, Simeon kissed the dragon on the forehead and hands.

The claws retracted, and scales faded away. Jane lay naked on the cold ground, in the rain.

The claw he held unclenched. Something cold fell into his hand.

"Jane!" he whispered.

"Oh! I have dreadful indigestion." She held her stomach. "Simeon, you recognized me. You rescued ... Simeon? What's happening to you?"

She rolled over and away from him, screaming. Dunkley's dogs scampered away from where Dunkley knelt, checking them over. They ran toward him, barking.

Puzzled, Simeon glanced down at his hand as the coldness spread into his arm from the thing in his hand. It was clawed and growing.

"Marishes!" he yelled. With his left hand he clasped his elbow. Panicked, he barely had the breath to say, *"The tongue of the Lord shall root out the deceit!"*

The dragon spell fed on his power and raced up his arm. The sleeves on his jacket and shirt ripped as the muscles underneath swelled. He howled in agony as his skin stretched. The dragon spell ran into his left arm. His own claws dug into his arm as he tried to contain the enchantment.

The stark scent of the battered yew burst over him, distracting him even more from his counter spell. Rain falling on the road and path nearby smelled dusty.

The clothes tormented him. He shouldn't be wearing clothes. He ran his razor-sharp claws down all the fastenings. The formal clothing fell away and he launched into the sky, roaring at the clouds. They broke apart and a sliver of weak autumn sun slid through the gray, as if embarrassed to be illuminating the day. His vast wings spread and covered the church yard, red and gold in honor of the sun. He was himself.

Something nagged at him: a tie to a feeble creature below. Angling his wings, he swooped low. Eyes like a telescope picked out the woman. She smelled of his kind. Turned, she had been a caricature of a dragon, but synapses primed to channel power let him work out how to correct her feeble stature.

Below, he sensed someone trying to summon back the rain. He sang his bass roar to the sun, and frightened it into shining.

Modulating his song, he called to the female, but received no acknowledgement.

What? That was *his* female. Someone must be preventing her from responding.

Back-winging, he set his legs on the ground and roared; his lashing tail smashed the dry-stone wall of the church yard. A tombstone toppled.

That female was his.

He stretched out his long forearms. Around him, three columns of light set up an irritating chant. He clawed the nearest one but it danced out of reach in a flash of brilliance.

In his belly, anger grew. He had to let it out. Roaring, the anger flared at the pillars of light. All three dived out of sight behind standing tombstones.

Satisfied they were subdued, for now, his full attention was on the woman.

One man, wearing colors of a faded sunset, stood between him and his prize. He lifted a great paw to swat the feeble creature out of the way.

"Simeon!" the man shouted.

He stopped. What was Simeon? Simeon was him. He set down his paw, twisting his head this way and that to better take in the man.

The faded-sunset man shook his head. "You need to take better care of your appearance. Have you seen yourself, Simeon?"

The dragon growled low in his throat. This was nonsense. He reached out a forearm for the woman.

The faded-sunset man lifted a mirror. "Look at you, Simeon!"

Still growling, he peered into the mirror. A dragon stared out at him. He glanced over his shoulder but no dragon was there. He peered into the mirror again. The eyes of the dragon caught him.

Look into the dragon's eyes and your illusions are stripped away. You see the truth—however much it hurts.

They were his eyes. This wasn't right. He wasn't a dragon. He lifted his forearm and inspected a heavily-clawed hand. It was a dragon's member and it was attached to him. He tried to back away, but something held him on the ground, one of the sneaky columns of light had snipped his flight feathers. He roared and thrashed his tail.

The woman stepped forward. "Simeon, please come back."

For her, he tried to remember. This wasn't his face. Peering in the mirror, he tried to remember a picture of Simeon. The shoulder-length, salt and pepper hair, the pale gray eyes swam into view. He pulled in his tail and, regretfully, his wings. Shivering in the cold day, he stood and stared in the mirror. His right hand remained clawed and scaled. The scales tried edging up his arm again.

Lifting his gaze, he saw Torquil holding the mirror. Panic lined his brother's face, but he stood his ground.

"Tor?" Simeon's voice croaked; his throat burned. He reached out to hold his brother.

"I know you won't hurt me no matter what your form, but …" Torquil gestured at the scaled and clawed arm that hung heavily off Simeon's shoulder. Simeon held out his arm to his colleagues.

Marishes laid his borrowed staves over Simeon's arm. *"They shall sow salt into the ground so that nothing can grow."*

The scales stopped growing at the point where the stave touched Simeon's skin.

Torquil's hands quivered as he held the mirror. "Why was he so huge? No disrespect, Jane, but without the tail you'd have fitted in a minibus. He could have *eaten* a jumbo jet!"

Simeon tried to smile; it was so like Tor to try and hide his fear in a joke. His throat ached too much to answer.

"It's a matter of power," Jane said, simple words stating the truth. "I'm a petty witch, Simeon is one of the most powerful and trained wizards of his generation."

"Ah! I'd be a lizard then." Torquil's voice held bitterness. So he *had* tried to use power. Simeon almost wept for the pain he heard in his brother's voice.

Dunkley set Torquil and Jane aside and stood in front of Simeon, gazing into his eyes. *"Speak truly, dost thou love the Lord?"*

Simeon's lips were swollen and his throat wanted to roar out the pain of the transformation to skies that clouded over again.

He forced his aching mouth to form the words he needed to say. *"The Lord himself is a portion of myself."*

Dunkley touched Simeon's cheek. *"Those that run after another god shall have great trouble."*

Simeon's teeth felt glued together. He closed his eyes and forced his lips to move. *"All my delight is in the saints."*

"Their drink-offerings of blood are altogether abominable," Dunkley said.

"The Lord is my cup." The coldness slid to Simeon's wrist

"Destruction and unhappiness is in their ways," Dunkley continued.

The pain in Simeon's throat eased. *"I thank the Lord for the warning given me."*

Simeon's right hand unclenched from the object that had fallen to him after he had rescued Jane. It tinkled as it fell on the gravestone. As Dunkley stepped aside and Simeon stood naked before the two people who loved him best in the world. He was human again, for them.

A small silver triangle had dropped to the tombstone. It was trisected with a 'Y'.

Simeon backed away from it. His feet tangled in the remains of his clothes. He hitched on his trousers; the fasteners were warped but the braces held them in place, covering his nakedness.

Trewithick removed his top hat and flicked the amulet into it using his cane. His colleagues peered in at it. Snatching up his ruined jacket and shirt and tugging on his clothes, Simeon joined them.

"What have we got?" Simeon asked.

"It's a Dragon's Eye," Dunkley said. "A triangle for threat and the 'Y' for the choice between good and evil."

"Where did you get that, Jane?" Simeon's fingers itched to hold it again.

"Penny gave it to me as we entered the church yard."

Her eyes roved over the church and graveyard until she found Penny standing in the shelter of the lych-gate. The limousine driver had a hand on her shoulder.

With a glance at the man, Penny stepped forward, head held like a queen. "You stand there, congratulating him on being a good dragon. But I did it; I made him into a dragon, nobody else."

Dunkley stared down the path at her. "Not entirely. You provided the form, but in order to—"

"Still lecturing, Dunkley?" The man stepped out of the shadow. It was David Green, once a brother but now living in the shadows.

"My brother and cousin follow their dreams of power but Penny sits at home like a good girl," she shouted.

Torquil slid his mirror away. "Foolish child. Do you know how many other people stand in your shoes? Consider my position; both my little brother and my lover soar among the powerful. They play with the power of the gods, but I stay with my feet on the ground, stealing snippets of joy from my lover's touch. My own father worships the ground my little brother walks on, disdaining his older son for the life choices I made."

"What forces you to walk in his shadow?" Penny said. "Their shadows?"

"I love them."

Simeon closed his eyes in relief. Torquil forgave his little brother for being more powerful.

"Then you are weak," Penny spat. She glared at her mother. "You ruined my life. Why should you be happy?"

Jane shrank away from the accusation. She pulled away from Simeon's sheltering arm.

"I had arranged a teacher for you, Penny," Dunkley said. "All you had to do was wait."

"As if I'd need a teacher you chose!" Penny raised her arms. "I found the teacher I need."

David Green patted her shoulder.

A cloud of the Darkness which Ends the Universe gathered about Penny's head. She shouted out, lowering her hands to point at Jane. She screeched some words in pig-Latin and two huge flashes of lightning arced across the sky. They joined above the church steeple.

Marishes jumped in front of them all with his borrowed staves crossed. "*I look towards the mercy-seat of Thy temple.*"

Simeon dug a hand into his brother's waistcoat pocket and snatched the mirror. He flung it in the air, as the arrow of plasma arced down—aimed straight at Jane.

"*For He is our strength and shield!*" Simeon shouted.

The lightning ran into the mirror, which shattered. Thunder deafened them as the shards fell until they hit Marishes's shield. As his hearing cleared, Simeon heard the tinkle of glass on the gravestones surrounding the group.

The rain, scared away by Simeon-Dragon, fell again, dripping on everyone.

He found he had curled, as had everyone, in that dreadful noise. He jumped to his feet, but not before Dunkley and Trewithick. They charged down the church path towards Penny.

She watched, her hand creeping towards the necklace about her throat. David Green muttered something and waved his hand. The pendant necklace glowed with anti-light.

Penny's horror cleared. With a triumphant grin, she fled with Green to the limousine. It pulled away, wheels squealing. The image of the vehicle flickered and vanished, but they heard the roar of the engine. Dunkley and Trewithick halted under the shelter of the lych-gate roof. As Penny had escaped, Trewithick walked to his car to place the amulet in a containment vessel. Dunkley stopped by the church porch and returned to the group with his Inverness cape, which he offered to Jane.

"She said I ruined her life." Tears ran down Jane's face as she clutched the cape over her nakedness.

Simeon didn't know what to say.

"At every wedding of our former Brothers there is always trouble." Marishes huffed. "Dunkley, we really can't have female relatives keep turning like this."

"I'm working on convincing the Council."

Torquil brushed leaf-mold from Marishes shoulder. "I've never watched you work before."

"I try to keep my home life and work separate." Marishes pursed his lips, prissy dancing teacher style.

Torquil trotted down the path to gather up the ruined blue dress. He shook it out. "Well, we'd better do something to salvage this wedding."

"Oh no, not now." Jane stared in the direction Penny had fled.

"But Jane…" A vice gripped Simeon's guts. Did she mean she wouldn't marry him?

"What was the necklace that Penny wore," Torquil asked.

"Black sorcery." Dunkley didn't look at Jane. "It's a control necklace. Green controls her."

"There! She was made to say that." Torquil glanced at all the faces and rested on Jane. "It's 'for better, for worse' and there's nothing worse than being transformed into a loathly dragon on your wedding day, so it has to get better from here on."

Simeon caught her hand. "Jane, please I ... Just please."

The horror, the rain, everything went away as he was lost in her warm brown eyes.

"Please marry me, Jane," Simeon whispered

Through her tears she stared at him. She must have seen something important in his face. "All right then," she said.

The pain in Simeon's stomach eased.

Before he could hug Jane, Torquil fussed her towards the church door. "As there's no bridesmaid, would you accept the help of an old queen?" Torquil hustled Jane and Marishes into the porch saying, "And I'll need your kilt pin to hold up this dress, Laird Alasdair, if you please."

Amusement lining his face, Dunkley unfastened the pin from his kilt and handed it through the door. He plucked a dragon feather he had stuffed in his belt and began to study it.

Simeon leaned his head against the cold stone of the porch as he tried to roll up the rags of his sleeves hung around his elbows. Not that anything would make his current attire presentable. "There's something you're not saying about Penny's necklace."

Dunkley fiddled with feather. "How did it feel to be a dragon?"

"This had better not be a side-track." Simeon clenched his fists.

Dunkley shook his head. "Tell me."

Simeon made a toss off gesture. "I was so powerful. I could do anything. I'd already worked out how to make Jane a more powerful dragon and we could repopulate Britain with our kind."

"So why did you give it up? You were powerful; the three of us couldn't take you down. Why drop the dragon's eye?"

Without thinking Simeon said, "Because it wasn't me."

Dunkley stared at the lych-gate. "Black sorcery requires conscious choice to let it affect you. At any point Penny can remove that necklace—if she chooses to."

The vicar burst from the church porch with Torquil.

"Horror of horrors, brother," Torquil said. "You've ruined the pen for signing the marriage register."

"It won't take two minutes while I run over to the vicarage and get a new one" the vicar said.

"No." Dunkley removed a dirk from his sock. With three strokes he sharpened the dragon feather into a quill pen and offered it. "This is more fitting."

The vicar accepted the new pen and hustled everyone inside. The human smells of cold candles and furniture polish washed over Simeon, grounding him.

Torquil and Marishes waited at the altar as witnesses, while Dunkley and Trewithick guarded the walk to the altar. He would have to find Penny before the Witch-Finders did and persuade her, for her mother's sake, to remove that necklace.

He took Jane's hand and she summoned up a smile, as barefoot and dressed in the rags of battle they walked up the aisle together.

Flaming Desire

Gillian heard the noise she was listening for: a car struggling up the track. She shoved the extraction hose in the trench and heaved on the starter cable: the pump thumped into life, spurting water into the new channel they had dug through the peat to drain the site.

Tired of the rain pounding on her head, she pulled the hood over her dripping hair. She rubbed her tired eyes, forgetting about the mud on her hands, and stretched her back. Yes, she recognized the people-carrier slogging through the river that now covered the road up to this remote archaeological excavation site.

"Is that the mysterious boyfriend?" Janice jumped back into the trench too early and splattered mud everywhere.

"I'll be back in a mo." Gillian waded down the drainage channel to the parking area; it washed the mud off her boots. The organizers of this dig had made an effort with gravel but the car still bounced through deep ruts. Behind her, Prof. Clacton made a similar move from his mound. As befitted his status as the boss, a marquee protected his trench from the rain.

Alasdair Dunkley peered out of his car at her approach. He opened the door and his two wolfhounds stared gloomily at the muck and persistent drizzle.

In her haste to beat the Prof, Gillian slid the last few meters. She staggered over to the car.

"You didn't mention it was this … rural." Dunkley said in his gravelly Scots accent. He reached behind him and slid open the back door.

She ignored the invitation to sit in the dry car. "I told everyone you were my boyfriend. I needed a reason for inviting you." That came out in an apologetic rush.

"I expect that's why your boss is huffing and puffing down here in unprofessional interest." He slid out of the car and pecked her on the lips—the greeting a long term lover might offer. They were nearly the same height. Her heart skipped as her lips clung to his, *if only this were real*.

"You're good at that." Oh no, she hadn't meant to sound disapproving. His beard was soft against her chin. When he released her, she saw there was more gray among the brown hair—even more than six months ago.

"One of the greatest counter-spells in our arsenal is True Love's Kiss: it breaks most personnel spells. It's rough and ready, but if you're in a hurry ... Well, I get a lot of practice." He glanced over her shoulder and malice glinted in his eye. "Believe me, darling, with the mud all over you I'm concentrating on your beautiful soul."

Gillian peered into the wing mirror. Mud covered her face and streaked her hair. Behind her she saw Prof. Clacton—in hearing range for Dunkley's last comment. At least the mud covered her blush.

"The pump keeps clogging up," she muttered.

Dunkley edged them both into shelter of his car and rummaged in the back. He produced some hiking boots, not as pristine as his complaint about the rural setting would have suggested.

As Dunkley changed out of his trainers, Prof. Clacton plodded to the car. Dunkley nodded a greeting at the incoming archaeologist. He stamped his boots to settle them on his feet and fastened an Inverness Cape over his jeans and sweater.

The hounds huddled on the other side of the car.

"I hope those dogs are trained," Prof. Clacton said.

Dunkley pulled the hood over his hair and faced the interrogation. "I could walk through a field of sheep without them being on a leash, but of course they wear a leash because it's the law."

Gillian stepped between the two men, interfering with the building staring contest. "Alasdair, this is my boss, Professor Ian Clacton. Professor, this is Alasdair Dunkley."

"We've met before," Prof. Clacton said.

"Yes, a discussion panel on 'Comparative religious practices in pre-historic settlements as shown in the uncovered artefacts', wasn't it?" Dunkley said.

O-oh! That didn't sound good.

The two men shook hands as if they each suspected the other of having leprosy. Inside, Gillian cringed. Maybe having two top professors here wasn't a good idea.

"Thank you for letting me visit this weekend. Once Gillian gets involved in one of these digs I don't hear from her for weeks." Dunkley tossed her a teasing glance.

"There's no mobile signal up here," she muttered, before remembering he wasn't a real boyfriend.

He lifted an eyebrow.

"Oh, I called you when Len and I went down to town to stock up on coffee."

"Well, now I'm here you can show off your mud pit." But he was smiling. He glanced at his dogs, huddled on the other side of the car to the open door. Ross lay down, indicating his lack of interest in the wet, outside world. "Och, you big softies."

Dunkley left the door open for them and joined Gillian and Prof. Clacton trudging up the muddy hill to the dig. He gestured Prof. Clacton to lead the way and hung back. Still doing the boyfriend act he took Gillian's hand to help her up the hill.

He glanced at Clacton then whispered in her ear. "So what's a respectable witch doing calling out the Witch-Finders?"

His breath thrilled her skin. She remembered to laugh and gaze into his eyes. "There's something off here, and I can't discover anything. This rain interferes with my link to the Fire Lady."

He kicked at the water in the drainage channel. "Running water short circuits my abilities as well, but I'll do my best. What got you suspicious?"

"Two people have gone missing." Gillian tucked under his arm. "The others act like they're in town to fetch milk."

"How long?"

"I've not seen them for three days. It's wrong. Am I reacting to the rain?"

"If you are, then I'm going to have two grumpy hounds. Please tell me you sleep in town or is it a sodding tent?"

Gillian stared at him through her lashes. "Sodden is the word you mean."

Dunkley laughed. It startled Gillian. When had they reached a point where they shared jokes? In his job it would be a bonus to get people on side quickly, but he was a great actor. They had met properly once before and had a casual acquaintance from work-related conferences.

"Ah well, let's go to work. *Surely thou hast seen it?*"

Something spread out into the ground. Dunkley studied the whole scene and his gaze settled on the marquee.

"This is my trench." Gillian patted her pump which had cleared the muddy puddle. Janice and Martin scraped the mud into buckets. Janice stared up at Dunkley with kitten-wide eyes. He ignored her.

"All this mud makes me glad I do my research in a library," Dunkley said.

"Without field work, you historians would have nothing in the library to research," the Prof said.

"For which I am eternally grateful." Dunkley lifted a mud-encrusted boot. "So what have you got under that marquee?"

"Some dog burials …" Prof. Clacton led Dunkley further up the hill to his mounds.

Letting them go on ahead, Gillian climbed into her trench. "Anything here?"

"That's the boyfriend?" Martin lifted his bucket of mud out of the trench. "I take it he's someone eminent. The Prof is acting like he's an intruder."

Gillian blushed. "Alasdair Dunkley, the Lecturer in Pre-history Religions at London University, a member of the Theological College."

Martin whistled. "You're a sly one. If you'd mentioned him sooner, it would have saved weeks of brangling when I was trying to access papers from their library."

There would be no working while everyone speculated on her relationship so Gillian continued up the path to the mound. Her head of department showed off his finds to her supposed boyfriend.

As she arrived behind them, Dunkley pointed to where Cheryl and Len were working. "But you've already got contamination on the site. That's a modern earring."

Prof. Clacton might have been a puffer fish. "So you're an expert on contemporary jewelry, are you?"

Cheryl screamed and fell backwards in her effort to get away from her assigned digging spot. Len peered at where Cheryl's trowel had dropped and jumped to his feet.

"No," Dunkley said. "It's still attached to an ear."

Archaeologists ran towards Cheryl's screams. Gillian put her arms around Cheryl to keep her from staring at the pale flesh in the dark earth. Gillian recognized that earring.

"Stand back, everyone!" Prof. Clacton shouted as he knelt down at the post Cheryl had vacated. "Somebody call the police!"

"There's no mobile signal here." Boris peered around Mandy like a ghoul.

Dunkley hitched up his Inverness cape and produced his phone. He checked the screen. "I've a signal."

"It must be a satellite phone to pick up anything; I didn't know they made them that slim," Boris said.

"Marvels of modern technology." Dunkley offered his phone to Prof. Clacton

Prof. Clacton wiped his hand on his waterproof and accepted the phone. "Right, everyone go to the canteen marquee. Boris, make sure no one leaves."

Gillian heaved Cheryl to her feet and Martin helped, practically carrying Cheryl down the hill. Dunkley remained with Prof. Clacton awaiting the return of his phone.

Someone had lighted the gas stove by the time Martin and Gillian man-handled the almost rigid Cheryl into the canteen marquee. They sat her in a folding chair and Mandy shoved a mug of tea into Cheryl's shaking hand. She spilled it but as she was still in waterproofs this didn't matter.

Mandy knelt beside the chair and helped her sip the tea. "What was it?"

"Did you see the earring?" Cheryl sobbed. "It was Julia's."

Mandy raised her eyebrow and Gillian nodded, lips a thin line.

Boris self-consciously guarded the tent door. "How long has she been missing? I can't remember her being around today."

"Neither she nor Lawrie have been at the site since Thursday morning," Gillian said.

The other seven people in the room exchanged puzzled glances.

"Are you sure?" Janice asked.

"Yes. I asked Prof. Clacton where they were and he told me they'd gone to town for the milk."

"So maybe the locals object to our digging in a special area or something," Boris said.

Gillian unfolded a camping chair and plonked down. Someone handed her a mug of tea and everyone sat, listening to the rain drum on the tent canvas.

"Should someone take the Prof and Gill's boyfriend a cuppa?" Mandy asked.

They all turned to Gillian.

"I don't know. Why haven't they come down here to wait with us?"

"Now that is easy, they have to guard the site to make sure nothing is touched," Boris said. "Don't look at me like that! They always say that on all the best cop shows."

Mandy got to her feet and poured out two more mugs of tea. "Right, Gillian, you take two mugs up there. We'll never learn what's going on, otherwise."

Gillian zipped up her waterproof again, even though the rain had slackened off. Trying not to spill the tea, she climbed the muddy track to the marquee.

Prof. Clacton saw her first. "You can't come up here."

"If you want tea, my dogs can guard the site for two minutes." Dunkley put his fingers in his mouth and uttered an ear-piercing whistle.

Two hounds burst out of the car and raced up the hill towards him. Once under the marquee they shook, spraying water over everyone's waterproofs. They trotted over to Dunkley, came to a halt in front of him and sat. Their heads reached his waist. He wasn't a tall man, a little over Gillian's 5'9", but they were still impressive. Dunkley ran a hand over their backs and whispered something to them. They sat in front of the dead body and watched.

Prof. Clacton stared at the dogs. "They're huge."

"Ross and Rory play at being impressive." He tugged his hood over his head and scrambled down to where Gillian stood in the rain. Prof. Clacton stood staring at the dogs until one of them growled, and then he rushed for his tea.

"As long as no one provokes them," Dunkley added, cupping his hands around the mug and sipping. Rain dripped off his cape.

Below them, police Land Rovers inched up the flooded track.

"I'd better get back." Gillian tramped down the soaking peat hillside. Once back in the marquee she said, "The police have arrived."

Even Cheryl had recovered enough to join the mad rush for the door. Gillian stepped aside.

How long would Julia have lain in the soil if she hadn't brought Dunkley in? She had noticed Cheryl move to work a little to the right of her allotted position to find the hidden body. Was Lawrie hidden in all that dirt or had he killed Julia and stashed her there before fleeing?

The group pushed back into the marquee and Prof. Clacton arrived with a police officer and Dunkley with his dogs. Dunkley put both mugs down on a table.

"Who is it?" Boris demanded. "Cheryl and Gillian both say it's Julia."

"We have yet to make a formal identification." The police officer took out a pad and pencil. "I'm afraid we'll have to close down the dig for a few days, while we go over the whole site. Has anyone been around the area that doesn't belong?"

All eyes went to Dunkley.

"Do you know, sir?"

"I'm the stranger." Dunkley unfastened his cape and slid his wallet out of his back pocket. He handed over his driver's license. "I arrived here this afternoon, at the invitation of my girlfriend, Gillian Blake."

The police officer took the license and his eyebrows hit his hairline. He handed back the card.

Dunkley put it away. "If you need further identification, I'm sure the University College where I work will provide you with a character reference."

"If circumstances merit it, Lord Alasdair, but I hope we can uncover the truth before that." He ran his eyes over the bunched archaeologists. "Gillian Blake?"

Gillian stepped out of the crowd. The police officer glanced at Dunkley, then back at her. She gritted her teeth against the obvious comparisons. Even with the concealing rain cape, Dunkley's body was super fit, while she enjoyed her dinner too much.

"I invited Alasdair here for the weekend, expecting neither the torrential rain nor a dead body."

Dunkley crouched between his dogs, who added a wet pungency to the air in the canteen tent.

"Did you have any particular reason for inviting a pre-historian to a pre-historical dig?"

"I didn't invite him to the dig. Of course, I hoped he might be interested." Gillian flushed, but she kept up the lie.

"If you're closing down the dig for a few days," Dunkley said. "Might we go to a hotel, rather than staying in a damp tent?"

The police officer eyed the rain outside the canteen tent door and wryly acknowledged the justice of that complaint. "I'm sorry. I do need all the archaeologists here to direct our search. If we disturb anything valuable, the museum will complain for the next decade, or more."

The police questioned everyone. Dunkley gestured Gillian to the tent door. She followed along; no one noticed as they moved away.

"Why are you going on about a hotel?" Gillian said. "My friend is dead."

"I was trying to clear the site of archaeologists."

Now she felt guilty for snapping at him. He tucked an arm around her waist and helped her down the muddy path. "Let's sit in my van and discuss this."

The clouds on the horizon were breaking up and the setting sun burned the clouds. A police dog sniffed at the ground under the marquee and barked. Ross and Rory lifted their heads, ready to chase off the intruder if given the command. Dunkley ran a hand over their hackles, directing them towards his car.

"At least the rain is slowing." That sounded inane even to Gillian. "It makes sleeping easier when the rain isn't pounding on the canvas."

Dunkley slid open the door on his people carrier and sat on the edge to remove his boots. Gillian slipped out of her waterproof trousers. She hung them over the wing mirror and left her boots at the door, underneath the car. Dunkley sat inside scrubbing at one dog with a towel while the other watched mournfully.

Seeing her, Dunkley tossed a second towel over. "Can you dry Ross?"

Dunkley pulled the door shut as the dog shifted to sit in front of her, with hope in his deep brown eyes. Ignoring that appeal was impossible.

"So what is happening?" Gillian toweled Ross. "I felt your spell."

"I use Practical Theology, not magic, so what you sensed was my prayer." A smile flicked over his face. "I have this argument with everyone. I noticed a spell keeping the diggers off that patch of ground so I cancelled it, with the problems that have now arisen. The police investigation will trample over our sort of evidence. We'd best conduct our search tonight. You know, sleeping in here might be possible. The seats fold down into a comfortable bed."

"Why are you complaining about a bit of damp? You're from the Highlands. It never stops raining there, according to my sister."

"You'll notice I live in London?"

Gillian gave up. "So we'll sneak around tonight?"

"One officer will remain on duty but one man is easy to bypass in the dark."

*****

A subdued gathering picked at their evening meal. Someone brought out the beer. Most people indulged, but Prof. Clacton and Dunkley drank tea.

Martin glanced over at where Dunkley sat next to Gillian. "I'm surprised an ordained priest is having an affair outside of marriage.

Gillian's face scalded, but she kept her eyes on her plate

Dunkley raised his eyebrows. "That's two interesting assumptions there."

"What do you mean?" Martin swigged from his beer can.

"The first, in order to teach at the college one should be ordained. As it so happens I am." Dunkley sipped at his tea mug. "But it's not required for all the teaching posts. Your second assumption? How do you know I'm not holding out on her until I can drag her to the registry office?"

"Surely the altar?" Cheryl said.

"As Gillian is a white witch, that wouldn't be appropriate."

Martin stared at Gillian. "Truly?"

"I've never hidden that I live in the coven at Lytton on Moor." Gillian said.

"Isn't that a problem?" Martin asked.

"It's probably against the rules, yes." Dunkley drained his tea and slid his chair back. To Prof. Clacton he said, "Thank you for the meal. I'm sorry to continue to intrude but the police asked me to stay, and I'm not about to abandon Gillian in this trouble."

He gathered Gillian with his eyes and they both left the table taking their dishes. They washed them in the hot water left on one side and put their dried plates away. Other people began slinking away, retiring early to their tents.

As Gillian and Dunkley left the canteen tent, the two wolfhounds rose from where they sat outside. Dunkley called them to heel and all four walked to the camp site, with the sun setting through clouds blown ragged by the rising wind.

"At least the wind will dry off the ground. Maybe it won't rain tomorrow." Gillian tapped on some taut nylon. "This tent's mine."

Dunkley had gone all quiet and distant. His eyes were defocused like they were watching something at the edge of the moorland.

"You aren't cross about the questioning are you?" Gillian burst out. "I'm sorry, I had no other excuse as to why I asked you to visit."

Dunkley refocused on her. It was like watching a marble statue or a painting come to life. He tucked an arm around her shoulder.

"I have no problem with being your boyfriend. I'll get my camping things and join you in here." He pecked her cheek. "Change into something you don't mind getting soaked. Waterproofs make a noise, and the ground is still wet."

Releasing her, he strode towards his van with the dogs racing ahead.

She watched for a moment and saw Dunkley retrieve two prosaic tins of dog food, setting bowls on the ground.

Reassured, Gillian crawled into her tent and changed into the thin cotton clothes she wore for digging in burning sun and pulled a fleece sweater over the top. She sat hunched up by the light of her camping lantern with the tent door hanging open to watch for Dunkley.

Some while later, Dunkley scratched on the tent wall. He had changed into jogging pants and tee shirt. She remembered him wearing those in bed six months ago.

"Aren't those your pajamas?" She cringed as she said it.

"Most of my call outs are in the middle of the night. I've never recovered from the embarrassment of wearing flannel tartan pajamas and being laughed at by a local Dark Lord." His words were as light and jokey as his previous manner, but his voice suggested he had gone back into his distant listening mode. He slid a padded mat into the tent along with his sleeping bag. He crawled in and sat on the sleeping bag staring into the dark outside the tent.

Gillian switched off her lamp. "When do we scout?"

"I heard a few rustlings in the dark as I walked over here. Perhaps another half an hour and everyone will be asleep."

He sounded unapproachable in the dark. His voice had no expression, just statements of fact. The half-joking lover-act was gone. Gillian hugged her fleece sweater around her chest.

One doesn't expect towering legends to have family, but Gillian's sister Sylvia had married Alasdair's cousin Douglas. Alasdair was best man and Gillian had been bridesmaid.

Alasdair had stepped in and stopped a psychic attack on Gillian at the wedding. That's when she learned he was a Witch-Finder, someone a witch should fear. But she didn't. The rest of the wedding party had assumed the best man and the bridesmaid had ended up in bed together.

It hadn't been like that but she could daydream. A gentle kiss while warm and sleepy was Gillian's favorite way to awaken. Alasdair was so handsome. He had a shy smile that made him more attractive to Gillian than the brash cousin who had married her little sister.

When he arrived here, Dunkley had done such a brilliant job of pretending to be a boyfriend. Her invented memory was strong in the dark. Gillian stared through the gloom at him. Maybe he'd be interested in reviving the boyfriend act for a few more minutes, while they waited. She slid closer to him in the dark and wrapped an arm around his shoulders. He was such a good kisser. His face was a white blur as he faced her. Gillian kissed him. His soft beard tickled her chin.

With an arm around her shoulder, he pulled her next to him on his sleeping bag. She moved closer.

Then …

"What am I doing?" She jerked away from him. He held her close.

"Don't worry, Gillian, I'll never take advantage of you."

"Yes, you told me that last time." Aarrrrggh! Stop sounding disappointed. She peeled his arm from her shoulder.

He ignored her comment. "Now, that's a subtle distraction. If we were what we pretended to be, then we would be occupied for the rest of the evening."

"I take it you used your True Love's Kiss anti-spell."

"Not at all. The sleeping mattress has prayers woven into it, disconnecting you from the earth. No elemental charm can touch you on here. Can you touch your Fire Lady?"

He was right; the Presence, which had warmed her even in the pouring rain, was missing.

"It's time to investigate." He crawled to the tent door and slipped his feet into his discarded boots.

Gillian hesitated. "Am I going to get all amorous again?"

"Do you still have the kilt pin amulet I used at your sister's wedding to break that spell?"

She reached into her sponge bag and pulled out a long silver chain with the kilt pin as a pendant. "I wear it as a necklace."

"Good idea." His hands fluttered on her skin as he fastened the chain around her neck. She tried not to lean in to his touch. "Keep it under your clothes, touching your skin. As long as you are aware magic is going on it should keep you safe." Dunkley stood outside the tent waiting for her. "The spirit here is a succubus and I'm … the best way to describe it is … allergic to succubae."

Gillian clambered out of the tent and stomped to settle her boots. "What?"

Dunkley stared up the hill. "We can scout out what's happening, but I won't be able to help. I'll have to call in Trewithick … Ah he's not available. Anyway someone else."

"Why? You are the Uber Witch-Finder: staying pure to better combat Evil."

"That's a convenient rumor to scare bad guys. This job leaves mental scars." The white of his face flashed her way. He forced the next words out. "It leaves me paralyzed when confronting a succubus. Trewithick used to stake me out like a goat."

"So why can't you call in this Trewithick?"

"When he tendered his resignation, he told me he'd reached the point where his only available course of action was to cower under his bed hoping the Creatures of the Night would go away: scars."

A tear tried to creep out. She scrubbed it away even though the dark would cover it. "I didn't realize your job caused so much damage."

"Better us than let the Creatures of the Night hunt the general population." He shrugged. "Trewithick's happy now. He's researching his latest series for the BBC." He set off up the path. A light glowed above the mound. They headed straight for it.

"Sir Nathaniel Trewithick? He was one of you?"

Dunkley lifted a finger to his lips as they approached the marquee covering Prof. Clacton's trench. A bored police officer stared down the track with a blank expression. Well, Dunkley had suggested it would be easy to get by him.

Close to the top of the mound, Dunkley dropped and belly crawled to the summit.

Gillian wriggled up beside him. Water soaked through her clothes but warmth from the Fire Lady spread into her limbs: a witch from fire coven never got hypothermia.

The warmth grew stronger as she peered over the top of the mound. The scene below was lighted by four burning braziers.

Between this burial mound and the next, five of the archaeologists were holding an orgy. The sight of fat Professor Clacton wallowing around naked made Gillian nauseous. Janice chanted nasty Latin phrases.

"Who are these people?" Dunkley whispered in her ear.

"Other than the Prof, there's Janice, Boris and Mandy. Martin's the one lying on the fallen stone with the Stone Age Venus on his stomach. That's a first in this country! We need to get it to a museum."

"I've dealt with one before, in Aberdeenshire."

"What! Why haven't I heard about it?"

"Shush now." His eyes darted all around the circle of light.

Gillian kept her eyes off Prof. Clacton and his miniscule equipment, but Boris! Under those baggy clothes he wore for digging, 'hung like a stallion' made a fit description.

Dunkley poked her. "Try not to get too interested or the lust spell will suck you in."

Gillian buried her burning face in the cold grass. "What are they doing? Aside from the obvious."

"How much do you know about black magic?"

"Nothing."

"Seriously?"

"Ellen and Thomas, our coven elders, say if we want to know anything about it we can go to the effort of researching it for ourselves. They're not going to teach us."

He continued staring down at the proceedings in hollow. "Interesting point of view. I teach black magic to students who pass the basic course. They have to know—"

"You're stalling."

"You're right of course, I am. The … Venus is a trapped air elemental. Given enough acts of this type, it will grant powers to the petitioners in the hope they will set it free. Janice is, I believe, the main beneficiary. She enthralled the policeman back there."

"I thought you did that."

He shook his head. "They are making up the 'worship' as they go along. From the general pattern here it appears Martin is the altar. He's … um do you really want to know what happens after this?"

The chant Janice sang increased in volume—along with the moans of arousal from Boris and Prof. Clacton. Gillian wanted rip off Dunkley's clothes.

"Tell me." Gillian clasped her hand around the pendant charm to ward off the lust spell—it stopped the action but not the desire.

"Martin is the altar. He's about to get raped and murdered." Dunkley slid back down the mound. "I can get someone here for tomorrow."

"What!" Gillian nearly screamed. Janice's chanting drowned out all noise up here. "You're cross about his questions."

"I can't help in this situation."

"We've got to rescue him!"

Before Dunkley held her back, Gillian pushed to her feet and raced into the circle. She slammed into Mandy's back, knocking her into Prof. Clacton.

He pushed her to the ground. His face glazed over.

Janice clutched at the Prof's hair and tried to tug him off Mandy. "He's mine."

Boris, eyes flaming with lust, wrapped his arms around Janice.

Ignoring them all, Gillian snatched the Venus off Martin's stomach and held it above her head. It was made of clay, not carved from rock as she had expected. Modern air elementals were trapped in stone gargoyles.

The participants of the orgy stopped their actions and crouched like wolves ready to pounce—especially the men.

She took a step away from them onto the collapsed stone they were using as an altar.

With the Venus gone, Martin's apparent paralysis vanished; he rolled over. He grabbed Gillian around the waist. "Get the goddess; we can use Gillian as the altar."

Heat burnt Gillian fingers, as if the statue had emerged from the firing kiln. She flinched and the Venus fell out of her slackened grip onto the stone slab. The clay shattered on the altar stone.

"You idiot," Janice shouted.

Martin released Gillian and back-handed Janice. "You let her reach the statue."

"No!" Gillian dropped to her knees, trying to fit the pieces together. "It was unique."

A roaring wind circled the hollow.

"Martin was right," Mandy said. "The Venus did call the practicing witch."

Free!" Wind swirled between the two burial mounds. Soggy leaves and broken heather branches lashed at Gillian's face.

"It doesn't matter now," Janice shouted. "Martin freed the anima when he knocked it out of Gillian's hand."

"Now what do we do?" Clacton demanded.

"FREE!" the wind howled.

Clacton opened his mouth but the wind stole his words. Above them the clouds twisted down in a funnel cloud.

Gillian flung herself over the pottery fragments. Mandy clung onto Boris who caught Janice in a tight grip. Martin and Clacton hunkered down. The funnel hovered two feet above Martin. His hair lifted over his head; he flattened on the ground.

The cloud sucked at Gillian. Then, gradually, the pulling eased off as the wind swirled higher and higher until it chased the clouds around the sky leaving a breeze at ground level.

"We've got to get it back," Clacton said.

"Give the spirit what it wants," Martin hand grabbed Gillian's ankle. "It called her."

Gillian kicked out and tried to crawl away, but Martin clung.

"Let's glue the figurine back together," Mandy said. "The ceramic cement is in the finds tent."

Gillian kicked out again and curled round, trying to pry open Martin's strong grip around her ankle.

The warmth in her soul that was the Fire Lady tutted at her.

"I didn't mean to," she whispered.

-Does 'meaning' matter? It happened. It must unhappen.

Where's Alasdair? Gillian thought.

"Where's that boyfriend of hers?" Boris asked. "If Janice's spell didn't work, he's out here too."

Martin pushed Gillian down and lay across her, his naked body and erection pressing against her.

"Get some rope!"

Mandy rummaged about in a pile of clothing and pulled the belt out of Clacton's trousers. She trotted over to Gillian and wound the belt around her arms and shoulders as Martin eased back.

"I saved you!" Gillian said.

"We set it up to catch you," Martin said.

Gillian tried to roll, but he hauled her onto the fallen stone they used as an altar. Then he lay across her legs as she struggled to get to her feet.

Boris leaned into her face. "Where's the boyfriend?"

Gillian closed her eyes and tucked her chin to her chest to blot them out.

Help me! Gillian thought. *Can you get Alasdair?"*

-You need to link with him.

Set up a link. The Fire Lady did that within the coven.

-He's trapped in his head. I can't get through to his rational thought.

Oh! He had mentioned he was unable to function around a succubus.

-It's going to need a blood link. In his arrogance he believes himself weaker than he is.

And belief was everything in this world. She had to get to him, but how? Clacton had brought his tie. With Martin holding down her legs, they bound her feet together.

Mandy reappeared carrying a jar of ceramic cement. "Do this fast. It's going to get away."

Clacton eyed the way the clouds were breaking up. While Boris and Martin still wore their arousal with pride, Clacton had withered.

Janice pointed at Boris. "Go find her boyfriend."

As Boris left she and Mandy pieced the statue together.

"Like that's going to work," Gillian said.

"Who left her ungagged?" Mandy said.

"What do you mean?" Janice asked.

"The creature is free, unless you know the specific bindings, it's never going to come back," Gillian said.

"How do you know this?" Janice said.

"Don't listen to her," Mandy said. "She's going to tell you she knows how to call the spirit back and will help us if you let her loose."

"We can't let her go," Clacton said.

Boris emerged out of the night, dragging Alasdair with him. The Witch-Finder was unconscious with a bruise on his forehead. "Silly little vicar has fainted at all the licentious activities. Hurry up, Janice."

He dumped Alasdair next to Gillian and sat down to sort out the pieces of the statue.

-Now make a blood link.

Oh, like I can move?

-Do something or you're both dead.

God, you're encouraging. Why can't you do something?

-Tell me what to do. I am limited by your imagination.

Truly? Gillian checked out the situation.

-Okay, the landscape is too wet to burn but I can do other things.

Boris flipped Alasdair's hand away from the ceramic shards. It bled onto his tee shirt. He must have cut his hand on the shattered Venus. A blood link, that's what the Fire Lady wanted.

-Ooo, I always had you pegged as one of the bright ones.

Quit the sarcastic commentary, if you can't suggest anything helpful.

-I await your prayers, oh dutiful priestess.

Gillian needed to be bleeding. And she needed her arms free. The revelers were piecing together the pottery goddess statue. She rubbed her hand against the edge of the laid stone. It hurt but she'd get blood.

Can you do a slow burn on this belt to get my hands free? She dragged her hand over the stone to the limit of her movement ability.

-Your wish is my command, the Fire Lady intoned.

A spark drifted out of the nearest brazier. Gillian watched it float through the night air and drop oh-so-casually onto the leather belt.

She smelled smoldering leather. Gillian kept scrapping her hand; she was going to get blood.

Next to her Alasdair groaned.

An artifact shouldn't be pieced together by committee. The volatile odor of the glue floated around the pot as Mandy pried off the lid. Clacton held out two pieces for her to paint.

"Those don't fit together," Janice said. "This bit fits onto that piece."

Boris laid out pieces in a line while Martin tried to set them out next a near match. At least their activity, however useless, meant they weren't watching her.

Boris shoved Alasdair hard to create more space for his line. He rolled over Gillian in a parody of a loving embrace. The cut hand dripped onto her fleece jacket. It was clotting, she had to get her own hand cut and the belt loosened before the blood flow stopped.

She dug deeper and her hand slid over the stone, her blood offering lubrication.

Can you speed that up a bit?"

-Certainly. With a potassium flare the belt snapped.

"What?" Boris jerked his head towards her. He leapt to his feet

Trying not to sigh, Gillian slapped her hand against Alasdair's. *Now can you create the link?*

-Working with a Witch-Finder will be unpleasant for you. Do you still wish to go ahead?

I caused this problem, I had better mend it.

Boris paused in a half crouch. Gillian stared then realized actions slowed when working at the speed of thought.

Dunkley's hand gripped hers 'til it hurt. She followed the pain and witnessed Dunkley's nightmare.

He kisses her. His lips press against hers. She remembers this from her daydream of earlier. They wake together and make love.

But she sees it through his eyes. Her flesh melts from her face. The teeth fall out of the rotting gums. Yet he is unable to pull away. He continues kissing her. Her clothes fall in tatters from her decaying flesh, but he is forced to kiss her skull. He pulls aside the rotting fabric of her trousers and lifts his kilt.

Gillian wants to break away, but she is held in his viewpoint by the link.

Her stomach churned, threatening revolt.

Warmth spread through her drawing a veil over the scene, settling her stomach.

What do I do?

-You must summon the deranged spirit and bind it. The Fire Lady sounded so calm and competent.

Umm, how do I do that?

-If I knew how to bind my own kind I would not need you to make a link with a Witch-Finder. The answer is in his head, find it. As for summoning the succubus—The Fire Lady sounded amused now—*Kiss him.*

What! Gillian wished that didn't make sense. She rolled.

Boris sped up too. "What are you doing?" he shouted.

Gillian pressed her lips against Alasdair's flaccid mouth.

His eyes sprang open. "Gillian? Are you real?"

His lips moved against hers but did she hear the words with her ears or in her head. Clouds gathered again. The tunnel cloud spiraled down.

"We need to bind the escaped spirit," Gillian said.

With an anxious glance at the threatening sky, Boris reached to pull them apart. Gillian wrapped her free arm around Alasdair to keep their hands in contact.

"Blood bond," Alasdair whispered. He must have realized their hands were already joined as he eased off on his grip. "Almighty Lord who called upon Philip and Bartholomew to become brothers, not by worldly custom but by faith, let us two here, Alasdair and Gillian, be joined as brothers by our blood."

-*Brothers*. The flames on the braziers danced as the Fire Lady sniggered. *You have to answer him, affirm the joining. Words set the limits on the deal.*

Prompted by the Fire Lady, Gillian murmured, "I give you all that is mine."

His surprise at her choice of words was clear through the mingling of selves: similar but not the same as when working with her coven; no blood-sharing had been involved with the coven, only the gift of the Fire Lady.

Gillian fought to retain a slight distance from him. His mind was a black hole, sucking her in.

Above her the terrible tornado stretched towards them. Boris froze again as her thoughts moved faster than action.

She scraped 'Dunkley'—as he thought of himself—away from her 'self', like scraping off mud but he clung to her as a sane spot in his nightmares. He was desperate to think of Gillian as a 'brother'. The idea of being in a link with a woman, while about to face a succubus, terrified him.

What do we do? Gillian asked.

Flesh peeled from her skin as Alasdair fought to bring his nightmare under control.

The wind stopped howling over the moor. The only sound came from the funnel cloud twisting towards them like an express train. Fire ran through Gillian's hands where they touched Alasdair's.

Terror burned in his heart. He scrambled to his knees, dragging her up with their hands still joined. Still holding her hand he raised it until it was covered, in a prayer-like gesture, by both of his. She slid her other hand over his, maintaining the blood link. She knew he felt her shaking. But so was he.

He leaned forwards so his lips rested on her fingers. She leaned in until they shared the same air.

Boris leapt for them.

And flew across the hollow.

The cloud swept down, encircling them. It brushed aside the other would-be witches, leaving Gillian and Alasdair in the calm center.

Gillian swirled into a dream. Sylvia, so thin, so perfect in that ivory wedding dress: the older sister in the ultimate humiliation of following the younger, more beautiful sister up the aisle as bridesmaid, not matron of honor. Alasdair supported his cousin Douglas at the altar—both men had eyes only for Sylvia.

Gillian remembered the dirt under her fingernails and how the silly green sheath dress highlighted her pudgy body.

Why does it have to be that way? the wind whispered.

Gillian became the ivory bride: beautiful, with her black hair flowing around her shoulders like a model in a hair care advert. Men whistled at her in the street as she passed. The bridegroom stunned as she arrived. The bridegroom? Alasdair.

The shock jerked her out of the dream.

Why should you be second? The wind rewove the dream. *I can make you more beautiful than your sister.*

She stared into Alasdair's blank eyes, not loving eyes. Fury ran over her skin like the wind.

Warmth and awareness spread through Gillian from the Fire Lady: the creature was desperate to lure in these two trained practitioners as worshippers. The others gave it little power: unless enthralled, they did not believe in spirits.

The succubus starved.

"The Fire Lady said you had the strength," she whispered. "See what is here."

Dunkley's hands clasped hers as the link swallowed her. He gazed at Gillian in the wedding dress. Again, her flesh peeled away. The skin rolled back from her flesh like a plaster peeled off. The skeleton kissed him. His horror clawed at her. The vision captured her, incapable of breaking free.

Gillian screamed.

Flesh fell from her bones. The wind whistled through the gaps, like a wind harp. She lifted skeletal hands around his neck. Her bare skull leaned in for the kiss.

In his vision, he stabbed her as her flesh melted away. Pain spread out through her rib cage and her breathing labored. His anger drove the stone knife further in.

Terrified by the anger, Gillian struggled to break the link. She needed to release his hands. Dunkley fought to keep his hands around hers—his contact with reality.

"Help me. Please."

She almost missed his whisper.

The succubus noticed something going wrong.

It locked onto Gillian's mind as she tried to break free.

Memories flowed over her.

Alasdair pushed her against the wall, feverously kissing her. His hands pushed up that silly bridesmaid's dress. He cared nothing for the Ivory Bride. He wanted her. She screamed for him to get on with it.

This didn't happen.

Her flesh melted away. Dunkley's powerful memories overwhelmed the succubus's induced images. The green dress crumbled into rags of moldering silk.

His past was a whirlwind of scenes. A small boy stood at the bottom of the stairs as a big man pushed a woman down the stairs.

"That will teach you to disobey me!" the man shouted.

The small boy ran to his mother's side and checked her pulse. The woman's neck was broken.

Dunkley's swirling memories pulled her in; one by one his friends fell away either dead or succumbed to their scars caused by fighting this Darkness. Around the edges she saw his hatred of the physical reaction to her body. She snatched at memories hidden in the darkness of his soul, pictures of people: dead people. Shame burned him that he had failed to save them. The names of every person killed by his hand etched a memorial on his soul; their blood scarred his mind.

She saw the whole man; pockets of sadness, a few parcels of joy. Tiredness bore him down; how much did his job force out of him? His eyes locked on hers. What he was seeing of her?

-Help him. Without your help he will never be free. The Warmth filled her with certainty. She knew how to defeat his memories.

Onto the skeleton he saw, she drew her plump flesh. She clothed it in the dirty clothes this body wore.

His mind tried to remember the melting flesh, but with the warm strength from the Fire Lady she held onto the boring image of reality. She added muddy waterproofs and the smears of dirt around her eyes from earlier. His panicked breathing slowed.

She let her mind merge with his. She needed to know how to bind this elemental.

And there it was, back at the beginning of his training. A tall man set out a vessel, and added blood.

Later memories swarmed in and the tall man threw himself over a cliff in madness. Madness which now sucked at Alasdair. Gillian forced him again to see boring reality—herself coated in mud.

Alasdair clung to the image, even though the mud tried to peel away and the waterproofs shred. Warmth spread through Gillian as the Fire Lady's power backed up her attempts to keep Alasdair sane. It gave Gillian time to work out what to do next.

First she needed a pot. She found the jar of glue. Fine, she'd use that.

She freed her right hand from Alasdair's slackened clasp. With a swipe of her foot she knocked the jar within reach and picked it up. Setting it between them, she tried to sort out the rest of the memory. It involved more blood.

"There's a dirk in my pocket," Alasdair whispered. His hands still clung to her hand as if she held him over a twenty story drop. He made no attempt to reach for the knife.

She reached into his pocket and took the dirk. She slid it between their joined hands, then she twisted the blade and jerked it out. From the new slash across their palms their mingled blood dripped into the glue jar.

"*Deliver me from the wicked doers,*" Alasdair gasped and, merged with him, Gillian echoed the words.

The familiarity steadied him, he had done this many times before. S/he/they saw the blood dripping into the pot, forming pools and rivers in the jagged swirls and hills formed by ceramic glue.

Still struggling for control, s/he/they drew on the Fire Lady's power through the link with Gillian.

Two voices spoke as one. *"The heathen are sunk into the pit that they made: in the same net they made is their foot taken."*

The lust crawling over Gillian's skin dripped into the pot with the blood. The succubus chased the lust.

Over the moor, the wind stilled.

Keeping their cut hands joined, Alasdair used his other hand to snatch up the lid of the glue pot. He indicated Gillian should hold the jar while he screwed on the lid.

"Thou hast put out their name for ever and ever." It was impossible now to tell who had spoken the words.

They knelt together, their left hands still clasped over the linking cuts. Around them in the hollow, Prof. Clacton, Boris and Martin lay still. Janice hunched over with her head protected by her arms. Mandy was nowhere.

From over the top of the barrow, flashing blue lights indicated the arrival of the police. The young officer left on watch must have summoned back-up.

"Let's get out of here." They slipped the jar into a pocket and they stood.

Police officers in high vis rain jackets swarmed over the mounds.

Too tired and confused to explain why Gillian should be granted a Witch-Finder's immunity, he whispered, *"I will walk innocently."* And she whispered it too, accepting that no one should see them.

They drifted away from the scene, without the police acknowledging their presence. The flashing blue lights lit their path down the hill.

At the canteen, s/he/they stopped and covered their joined left hands with their right hands. *"Go in Peace, in the name of the Lord."*

He released her hand.

The comfort of his knowledge and experience slid away from her. She sank into a chair and stared up at him. "How did I dare to try that?"

With the link to the Fire Lady's strength gone, lines of exhaustion etched into his face. Without any more words, he headed down to his car.

He took her heart with him. His sense of duty forced him to perform the ultimate requirement of his job—killing people. Yet he was the kindest person she had ever met. He was the most alone person she had ever met.

Once again the Fire Lady flared in her head. -*There goes the greatest living Master of the Dark Arts. You heard him admit knowledge of Black Magic. If you let him walk away then you and you alone will be responsible for what is to come.*

"What?"

-*You are the one to keep him from falling into the Darkness.*

"No pressure then," Gillian snapped.

-*Well, if you really don't want to try. But it will be such a faff to get someone else from the coven into the position of trust you hold with him.*

"He doesn't need a lover, or want one."

-*Do you love him enough just to be his friend?*

Gillian stared after him. If she was honest with herself, the whole business of calling him her boyfriend had been to give him a hint she wouldn't be adverse to the idea. Now she had witnessed his soul she knew there was no way he would let that happen. The cold loneliness of his life had played out before her.

He needed a friend who wouldn't be killed by the creatures, or become scarred by that lifestyle. Yet one who knew who and what he was so he could talk freely. The Fire Lady was right.

Gillian ran down the track after him. "Alasdair, wait!"

He halted and half-turned back to watch her slipping after him

"So where is this mythical hotel in town you keep talking about?" Gillian said. "How about we pretend we slipped away for a night of passion together and reappear in the morning in all innocence? I would do anything for a hot shower right now."

He hefted the glass glue pot containing the succubus. "If you'll let me stow this, I'll help you collect your bag."

On the hillside above, the police were distracted by restraining the mad people who had killed Julia in a weird sacrificial ritual so they failed to notice the car slipping away.

Dark Service

Mike Rider needed a cup of coffee. Standing under a streetlight, he squinted at his watch—twenty minutes until Midnight. Noticing the smoke stain on the back of his hand he tried to scrub it off on his scorched jeans. The dirt smeared a bit further.

If he went into the nearest Starbucks covered in soot and with his leather biking jacket blistered from intense heat, someone might call the police. Without the backup of the college—he'd resigned due to their complete inability to modernize—he would have a hard time explaining about the invasion of Fire Bugs at the archaeological dig next to the wall.

Not the migrant firebugs from the US that ate lime trees—the other sort.

A group of youths playing with an immature fire elemental attacked tourist sites by generating magically flaming beetles. He had stopped them for today and imprisoned their fire elemental. The burning had stolen the air from his lungs and left his throat feeling like five days in a desert. He required caffeine before his homeward journey.

There was one coffee shop he frequented during the day. At this time of night their different style of customer might be less inclined to be pleasant. However coffee needed to be had.

Mike followed the siren call through the darkened snickleways. Down here, no one remembered to change the blown light bulbs. The coffee house stood deep in the maze that was the oldest part of York. There had been a coffee house on that site since the 1700s but you would never find it these days, unless you happened to live an alternative lifestyle.

And there it was: Isabella's.

In daytime, he brought Sally, Timmy and baby Trudy to this café. Sometimes he met friends here, from the old days when he worked as an Inspector for the Church Office of Misuse of Cræft— Witch-Finder for short. At night the place had a darker atmosphere.

Isabella's: the name resonated with the local Dark Side.

He trudged down the steps to the basement and opened the door. The sweet smell of coffee and chocolate billowed into Mike's face. The coffee house was unlicensed—so no alcohol was sold here—but the air was almost the pick-me-up he wanted.

Chattering clientele sat around wooden tables. Mirrors on the walls picked up the light from LED flickering candles, but not the faces of some of the customers. On the wall over the mantelpiece—a real fire, complete with bubbling cauldron—was a framed portrait draped in black of the witch Isabella Billington, burnt at the stake in 1648.

On some tables, scented geraniums grew in pots of local soil. On other tables the proprietor arranged bunches of Basil, Chamomile, Lemon Balm and Lavender in vases of water. Overhead, two ceiling fans mixed the natural perfumes to create a calming atmosphere.

Maybe no one would notice him. He stepped inside and closed the door. If he could use a misdirection … but then no one would notice him waiting to be served.

There was no queue; good, he had a chance of making it out alive.

He took three quick strides from the door before someone at a table nudged their neighbor and pointed.

Stillness spread over the café. Mike's knuckles whitened around his hiking stick. He kept walking. Five more steps to the counter, four more …

"What the devil are you doing in here?" A man pushed up from his seat near the fire. His hand headed towards the long pocket in his coat holding his wand. Mike knew the pocket was there because last month he'd faced down this man over allegations he was growing enriched Belladonna in his allotment, intending to drive off the tourists by giving them heart attacks.

Mike kept walking.

Another man stood up, his wife behind him, blocking Mike's route to the counter. Their fern collection had forced the evacuation of three Riverside hotels in a recent flash flood.

"We don't want your sort in here," the man said.

A woman jumped to her feet. "Better than your sort. If Mike didn't stop you, I'd have no tourists visiting York to buy my scented candles. It's not like you purchase your ritual equipment locally. Rumor says you source them off the Black Forest website."

The fern collector defied the candle maker. "So what if I do? Your prices are extortion."

The candle maker hitched up her sleeves. "My prices reflect the work gone into crafting a reliable product—one that avoids exploiting the voodoo workers in Haiti!"

"You wouldn't want them as customers." Mike recognized a calligrapher who worked by day as journalist at the local paper, by night he sold written spells. "They don't pay their bills on time."

The candle maker reached for her elemental energy from the fireplace, as the fern grower was summoning an earthquake from the energy in the soil of the plant pots. The calligrapher dabbled his fingers in the water from the flowers.

Before anyone grabbed the energy from the zephyrs being thrown around by the ceiling fans, Mike swung around. He raised his staff high. Anger, built up from having his dinner interrupted to fight some magical vandals, burst out of him in a vicious prayer.

"*The Earth trembled and quaked: the very foundations of the hills shook and were removed.*"

Everything became flat and still—for Mike it felt comfortable. He had isolated the whole building from the Earth and all nature magic required a link with ground. No one in this building was able to summon the smallest hint of elemental magic.

"I just came in for a coffee," he shouted into the stunned silence and leaned his hiking stick against the counter. Laying a fiver on the countertop he said to the server, "I guess I'll take that to go."

Circles of Hell

Felicity crouched to tie the ropes to the plank. Around them the midnight moon streaked the countryside in stark white and shadow. Staring at Josh with studied innocence she said, "Not all the patterns are made by human intervention."

"I'd heard something of the sort." Josh rubbed his mouth failing to hide his smile. "What do we do now?"

Her brother, Hartley shrugged off his backpack and set it down next to the gate. Pulling out a cap with a sighting hoop dangling off the peak, he tucked his frizzy curls inside. "We walk up the tramlines and choose our spot for tonight's picture. I've designed a flower."

He unfolded a sheet of graph paper. Curious as well, Felicity stood. Squinting in the stark-light of the moon, she imagined it laid out on the field. Shame it was such a small circle; a field this size would take a giant squid, one to rival that jellyfish that made all the papers.

"What about the photos of those great fractal patterns?" Josh said.

She heard the disappointment in his voice.

"A large cadre is needed to make a pattern that hits the news," Hartley said.

"I'll suppose staying in the pub with your mate has more interest now," Felicity said.

"It was going to be yet another early night if I had. We're on a walking holiday," Josh said.

"Why with him?" Felicity hoped in the dark the blush wouldn't show. She added hurriedly, "Is he your father?"

Josh sniggered. "Me Da is in prison for beating up his second wife, I think. Me Mam won't tell me much. Mr. Dunkley is my tutor. I've got to do something in the summer vacation or me Mam will have me working graveyard shift at the local chippie—why people can't get the munchies at normal times I don't know."

Hartley toed the backpack on the ground. "I've got a midnight snack in my pack for later."

Felicity leaned on the field gate. "You never told us what you're studying, Josh."

He glanced at her sideways. "Theology."

"You! Going to be a Priest! Never!"

Hartley rolled his eyes. "Lissy! I'd shut it before sticking your other foot in. I'm sure we're on a ley line here. What does your book say, Josh?"

Josh slid a pen torch and a map book out of his pocket. Cupping his hand over the torch to focus the light, Josh studied the book. "There might be an old trackway here." He flicked off the light and slid the book and torch back into his pocket.

"I note the change of word. You don't believe in ley lines then?" Hartley asked. He climbed over the gate and studied the area.

Josh leaned on the wooden rail. "A lot of mysticism has been added to a network of utilitarian Stone Age traders' pathways."

Hartley pounced, as Felicity knew he would. "What about the tracks that line up with the rising sun?"

Josh threw back his head and laughed. "Got me! But the archaeology suggests they were added later."

Hartley opened his mouth to argue.

"Are you really going to be a priest?" Felicity lifted the back pack over the gate and climbed over to join Hartley, who glared at her for the interruption. Huffing, he turned his back and sighted out the ground.

"Can I borrow your hiking stick, Josh?" he asked.

Josh handed it over. "If you twist here and here it opens into a long staff."

"That's handy," Hartley said. "It saves me having to find a straight enough branch." He stalked down the tramline to insert the stick in line with a tree. He backed up, testing the sighting.

"Hand that board over, will you?" Felicity said.

Josh lifted the plank over the gate. He caught Felicity's hand as she reached for the wood.

"I'm not a Catholic, Felicity," he said as Hartley walked back. "I'm Church of England. They're called vicars not priests. Is there anyone over there, Hartley?"

Shaking his head, Hartley unhooked the bundle of ropes from over the gate. "You're studying to be a vicar? Why were you reading a book on ley lines? Surely you're against pagan ideas."

"Know thine enemy." Josh stepped back, and then he vaulted the gate.

Felicity gasped at this show of fitness.

He touched down on his toes at the other side. He was a man comfortable in his own body. He walked like a wolf, not hunting but prepared if dinner appeared.

"Not what you expect from a vicar?" he said, a hint of smugness in his voice. He was showing off—Felicity tried not to be pleased he was showing off for her.

Snatching up his backpack, Hartley walked further up the tramlines. He grabbed Josh's hiking stick as he walked past.

Felicity ran ahead, the waving wheat ethereal in the moonlight, the rustling like a snake's scales in long grass. At times like this she wanted to dance. She ran her hands through the bowed heads of the crop.

Hartley didn't hurry. Josh slowed his pace to follow and frowned slightly. He bent to peer between the stalks. He darted a glance at the moon, then back at the ground. Lowering his plank he crouched and, with his penlight, studied the soil. He picked up a stone.

"Chalk land here, is it?" His deep voice carried on the lightest breeze.

"What say there?" Hartley said

Josh hefted his lump of stone. "Chalk, and lots of it."

"Usual around here." Hartley took the stone from Josh. "The clay soil shows it up well."

Felicity trotted along the tramline towards them. "We need to get finished before dawn you know."

Hartley dropped the stone and Josh ran his penlight over the ground. It was littered with irregular lumps of chalk and flint. He slipped the light back into his pocket. "Are there many burial mounds around here?"

"This is a whole sacred landscape," Hartley said. "Most of them are ploughed under. Have we got one here?"

"It's a possibility," Josh said. "Okay, where do we want to start?"

The pushed on until they reached Felicity's spot. Again Josh checked the ground. There were more of the stones here.

Hartley lined Josh's hiking stick up with a hill. "I keep the loop on my hat in line with the staff and that hill, and then I get straight lines."

"And my part in this is?" Josh asked.

"Follow orders," Felicity said. "That's what I get to do when Hart's on the team."

Behind Hartley's back Josh grinned at her.

Her stomach clenched, in a good way, at the mischief in his face. She liked the way he caught his hair back in a plait. Not as long as his tutor's but still…

He wasn't the sort to preach sermons on a Sunday in a stone box closed off from the Earth and Sky. He was too *Real* for that.

"First, we dedicate the ground," Hartley said.

Josh spread his hands in a go-ahead gesture. Hartley put his backpack on the earth and crouched next to it. Lifting out a rain mac, and a packet of crackers, he rummaged until he found a bottle of red wine and a corkscrew.

With a grunt Hartley heaved out the cork. "We'll drink the rest later. With the snack." He tipped a couple of tablespoons of wine into a plastic cup and dug the bottle into the ground.

He paced up the tramline and then jumped into the crop. He poured the wine on the ground.

Felicity inched up to Josh as they watched Hartley. "There are other ways of dedicating the ground you know?" She gazed at him from under her lashes.

"Hmmm?"

"Perhaps I can show you later?"

"Perhaps," Josh said.

Despite his discouragement, she noticed his honest speculation. She was glad she'd worn the hot pants as she watched his gaze travel up her legs.

Hartley strutted back to where Felicity and Josh stood.

"Have you hurt your ankle again?" Felicity said. "I've warned you before about jumping like that!"

"Right." Hartley watched the place where he had poured the wine. "Get those boards; we'll work on the stem first. From here it'll curve round that way."

Felicity slipped off her trainers.

"Is that compulsory?" Josh asked.

She shook her head. "I want the earth between my toes."

It was times like this when she was truly alive with the thrill of being in touch with nature. Then she grabbed Josh's arm. "Get your plank and we can start."

Walking side by side almost touching, Josh and Felicity created the stalk as Hartley directed their pace from the tramline.

"So you don't believe in the power of ley lines?" she asked Josh.

"I find it difficult to believe that power flows in defined rivers. If there is power, it should be everywhere." He spread his hands, encompassing everything.

It must be his church training, she thought. *On nights like this the power runs over me, like paddling in a chill river on a summer's day.*

The stem finished below the spot where Hartley had poured the wine.

Josh crouched and checked the ground again. Felicity saw the lumps of rock he and Hartley thought came from a barrow.

Hartley directed them to place their boards for the circle in the center of the daisy—circling around the dedication of the soil.

Josh stood and joined her. His swung his head around as if trying to locate something.

She stretched her neck to see what he was looking for but saw nothing. They pulled their boards around in unison, but Josh's steps slowed, as if he was wading through treacle.

As the circle was completed, his head jerked up. He launched himself at her and together they rolled out of the circle. Landing with her on top.

"What the—" she shouted.

Soil pelted her. The two planks of wood launched skywards on a fountain of mud. *Something* exploded up from the ground in the center of the circle. Long root-like tendrils burst into view reaching for the bright moon.

Josh pushed her off. Rolling to his feet, he stood between her and whatever it was. He tugged a mobile phone from his pocket and touched the speed dial button.

From the ground, Felicity watched a root tendril slam Josh across the chest. He rolled with the blow. His mobile flew out of his grasp, falling near her.

Her brother lifted his hands and sang out words in an odd language that stung her hearing. She slammed her hands over her ears as more roots erupted skywards.

The stench of stagnant water blew over the field. Felicity gagged—it burnt the skin in her throat.

Back on his feet, Josh snatched his staff from the sighting point. He backed away, tugging at the rubber ferule on the end to reveal the spike. Felicity lay there with her mouth open.

"Josh? Is that you?" A sleepy voice sounded near her hand.

Felicity fumbled Josh's phone to her ear. "There's a thing here!" she shrieked.

A root slapped her across the face, and the phone went flying into the wheat stalks. She landed face first spitting out soil.

A root swiped over her head, the crop bowing before it. She tried to get to her hands and knees to scramble out of the way, but another root slapped her backside and she sprawled in the dirt again.

She rolled over and another root slashed at the air above her— she heard the crack of air like a whip.

"Help!" she screamed.

At the circle, Josh stabbed at the roots with the spike of his stick. He twisted it, ripping one into shred. But each shred became a new twitching tendril.

"Felicity," Josh shouted. "Run!"

Hartley shouted something in that odd language. A rush of ickyness slid over her on the way to Josh.

"Hart—" But the roots weren't attacking him. He waved his hands, like a conductor directing the way they moved.

Panting, Josh jumped another root like a skipping rope, and shouted, "*He came flying on wings of the wind.*"

A fresh smell, like mint, settled on the field. The trees on the edge of the field rustled, then roared like waves crashing on the shore, but here in the field the air was still.

Slashing at another root, and then stabbing into the center, Josh shouted, *"At the blasting of the breath of thy displeasure."*

Another gentle fizz—like almost flat cola—spread out from Josh. He freed a hand from the staff, made a gathering gesture over his head and pointed into the center of the root explosion.

The wind caught in the trees and poured over the field, stealing Felicity's breath. The roots shrank from the onslaught, lashing and pounding on the ground.

Hartley shouted something over the raging torrent of wind and raised his hands. The air stilled, growing fetid, clammy. The roots stretched out new tendrils.

Hartley sang out a harsh, wordless note three times. The wax in Felicity's ears ran liquid.

She scrabbled to her feet, but the ground shivered under her. It rolled, toppling Josh.

With a dreadful shriek the ground opened up; a slit became a crack then a chasm running towards Josh.

"Let not the pit shut her mouth upon me!"

With a stroke like an angel's feather, the ground shut and Josh rolled onto his knees. He pointed his hiking stick at Hartley. *"All Kings fall down before him."*

This time it was a hammer blow, like the chime of a chisel on fresh marble, slamming Hartley in the back of the knees by some invisible force. He collapsed.

Occupying the landscape like a young god, Josh swept his staff in a gesture that covered the field and again pointed it at Hartley. *"Their eyes shall swell with fatness!"*

The crops bent as his staff passed over. Dust and pollen swirled around Hartley. He sneezed, and then croaked out some words with tears rolling down his cheeks. The words crawled out of his mouth like primordial slime and Felicity's skin broke out in a nettle rash. But Hartley's face and voice returned to normal.

Is this what power is like?

Once again the roots reached out. Instead of indiscriminately slashing, they coiled around Josh's feet like a python.

"Let us break their bonds asunder!" Josh shouted.

The joy of his words failed to break the grasping tendrils. Hartley shouted too, drowning Josh's voice. The roots coiled up past

Josh's knees. They couldn't be roots! They grew sharp thorns which dug into Josh's flesh. Dark liquid soaked into his trousers.

In a high singsong voice that didn't belong to him Hartley said, "The Earth Lord says you're a Nature Hater." He climbed back to his feet. "He says I've got to kill you."

This had gone far enough.

Ignored by all parties, Felicity crawled through the wheat bent over from the forces the men were casually chucking around the field. She reached the tramline.

Glancing over her shoulder, Felicity saw the roots had crawled up to Josh's hips. He battered at them with his hiking stick. His voice cracked as he shouted, *"They are like the chaff which the wind scattereth from the face of the Earth."*

The trees rustled, but nothing more. The stench of stagnant swamp rolled over the field again. A cloud crept over the moon.

"Cast away their cords from us," Josh said, panting.

Hartley face slid into a smile—a trick of the light turned his teeth in to fangs. He sang out a chant in his mad, shrill voice.

Under cover of this noise Felicity reached for a rock. She had to shut Hartley up. Her hand found the packet of crackers next to Hartley's pack.

That was it! She had the very thing to stop up his mouth without even hurting him.

A fingernail snapped as she scrabbled at the packaging, then she managed to rip open the packet of crackers. They spilled out over the soil. Sneaking another glance over her shoulder she saw Josh trying to pry the roots off with his stick. Even his shirt was stained in dark liquid. She grabbed one of the crackers and smeared it with butter from the stoneware crock Hartley insisted on carrying.

For a moment she debated trying to find the pâté, and then she shook herself. Why had she even bothered with the butter? Habit. A dry cracker would work as well.

The awful chant emerging from Hartley's lips lifted the hairs on her spine. His attention was all on gloating over Josh.

Creeping up behind him, she stuffed the cracker into Hartley's open mouth.

The chant spluttered to a stop.

"Hartley! Stop this nonsense!" Felicity said.

Hartley swung around to face her, spitting out buttered cracker.

But Hartley wasn't there.

His eyes were totally black and his face was blank. He showed no recognition of her. Felicity backed away.

"Hart?"

Behind her, Josh shouted. *"Thou shalt bake them in the fiery oven in the time of thy Wrath."*

The air tingled again and heat washed over her from behind. She took another step away from Hartley. This wasn't like her brother at all. Maybe it wasn't him. But possession was just in horror stories, wasn't it?

Hartley whispered words she didn't understand in that unnatural voice.

This game had gone far enough.

"Hartley!" Felicity dashed forward and slapped at his face.

He caught her hand. His palm on her wrist burned as he gripped hard enough to crush the bone.

With her other hand, she grabbed his thumb and wrenched it back.

He howled and for a moment Hartley flickered back into his face. His grip released and she tugged her arm away with such haste she fell onto the backpack.

Hartley's strode towards her, the blankness back. His hands lifted in a petition to higher things as he chanted, high and clear.

The air refused to be inhaled. She gasped, one hand to her throat. Black crept into the edge of her vision. Her groping hand found the butter dish. With huge effort, she chucked it at Hartley. The lid flew off the base and landed in the dirt, but the base, with the butter, cracked on Hartley's temple.

His eyes opened wide, that terrible darkness clearing. He keeled over.

The air rushed back into her lungs. With sobbing gasps, Felicity scrambled over to her brother as two huge dogs bounded past her. She would have expected baying, but their silence was terrifying.

"Break them into pieces like a potter's vessel," Josh's voice was calm now.

Something in the fields crashed, as if someone had smashed a vase. She buried her face in Hartley's chest. Shards stung her neck and bare arms.

"Oh you're here are you? Ross Ceart!" Josh said. "Rory, Cearr!"

One of the dogs snarled and Felicity lifted her head. The dogs split up, left and right, to circle the thing. The roots that had captured Josh were gone, but more were growing. They were slower without Hartley to order them.

"*Cum air ais a.*" Josh stabbed the spike of his hiking stick into the center of the roots again. "*He thundered down from the Heavens.*"

More wind howled over the trees. As she ducked her head from the onslaught she saw another man leapfrog the gate and run towards them.

The wind tried to tear her from the ground. She clung to Hartley. Yet the second man walked through the storm. He crouched at her side and touched Hartley on the throat. Under his leather biking jacket she saw a pajama top, and his feet were bare.

"Is he dead?" Felicity gasped.

"Did you want him to be?" the man asked with a slight Scot's accent.

Felicity sat up straight, all her fear forgotten. "He's my brother, thank you very much."

"He's alive. Are you all right?"

It was Josh's tutor—last seen at the pub.

"Fine! I... Josh?"

She scoured the field for Josh. He danced with a whirlwind. Ecstasy lighted his face from within. If he had taken the aspect of a god earlier, now he was creating the world.

"What's happening?" she whispered.

As she watched, the whirlwind died. The inhuman joy faded and Josh's face was lined with exhaustion.

With the fight over, he checked for Felicity and noticed his tutor had arrived.

"You took your time getting here," Josh said, but he was smiling.

"You hardly needed me." The man helped Felicity to her feet as Josh strolled over. Hartley groaned.

"You do that too? Casually play with that sort of ... of ... stuff!" She snatched her hand away from the second man. "What was Hartley doing joining in? He's never done that ... stuff ... before!"

"Thanks for stopping him." Josh grimaced. "If Felicity hadn't nutted him with the butter dish I'd have been a goner."

"Never underestimate any help you can get. Ross, Rory, *thugainn thu.*"

The dogs stopped sniffing at the circle of flattened wheat and trotted over. "And *Gaidhlig* sounds lousy spoken with a Yorkshire accent."

"What happened here?" Felicity screamed. "You're acting like it's normal to have the earth attack people!"

The cloud uncovered the moon and she saw a pattern in the flattened wheat—a giant squid with root-like arms flailing around as the wind blew over the field. Just like the creature in the soil. Trembling, she stared at the little circle where the creature had appeared.

Josh gestured at the field. "You told me yourself some crop circles weren't made by humans."

Freezer Burn

Pitkeathly stood outside the solid oak door clicking his fingers. Maybe Mr. Kilbride wasn't in …

"Herein."

Pitkeathly cracked open the door. Peering around the edge he said, "Sir, Mr. Dunkley told me to report to you today."

"He did?" Mr. Kilbride stared at his paper-strewn desk and picked up a letter decorated with the heavy college letterhead. As he pressed into the room Pitkeathly saw the paper was covered in the spider-fallen-in-an-inkwell handwriting of Mr. Dunkley—Lord Alasdair really, but the College was a bit silly about ignoring titles.

Mr. Kilbride—who Pitkeathly knew was the Honorable Edward, younger son of an earl—laid aside the letter. He rummaged in his piling system and retrieved a pile of progress reports from Mr. Collier.

Pitkeathly stood straighter in his Savile Row suit; he knew how glowing the reports were. Their fulsomeness embarrassed him sometimes when he knew his Uncle in the High Council read them.

Kilbride flicked through them with a sour expression on his face. "Oh fine! As if my life hadn't got enough excitement in it with those ruddy ghost sheep last week that were nothing of the sort, now I'm assigned a tutoricide."

"I say, sir. That's not fair! You sound like I pushed Mr. Collier down the well full of angry water nymphs. It's not as if I did an Analay. I rescued him!"

Mr. Kilbride tipped the reports one by one into the bin and stared at Pitkeathly, who shifted from foot to foot. He dropped his gaze first but Kilbride's stare burned into him as he watched the falling paper until a line in Dunkley's letter caught his eye.

... prove his value or get him out—fast.

The words tore at him. He'd almost exploded with pride when he learned he'd been reassigned to having a tutor who was one of the Cardinal Angels. Even his Uncle had patted his shoulder. Under that level gaze it felt presumptuous to consider he was worthy.

"I wouldn't try that sort of insubordination, yet lad. Mr. Analay has earned the right to question the senior members of staff."

"Sorry, sir." Pitkeathly stared at his handmade shoes. They wanted him out. Why? All he ever wanted was to fight the demons. One day he too would take down a dragon single-handed like in the stories Uncle Fuller had told him at bedtime.

Mr. Collier thought he was good but Mr. Dunkley didn't believe the reports.

"We've all done pratfalls. I heard Collier had decided to take a holiday in Death Valley to recover." Kilbride sniggered. "Anyway, you're a second year, hey? Well, we'll see how you go. There's a haunting I'm assigned to. I hope you've worked hard in the gym. Let's get some 'exorcise'."

Slamming his hand down on the desk Kilbride pushed to his feet and strode to the door. He grabbed the hiking stick that was shoved into a brass umbrella stand.

Pitkeathly scuttled after him. Now he would get to prove how good he was.

As they strode out of the front door, the porter brought their coats. Kilbride flung on his coat, accepted his hat from the porter and strode out.

"And here is your staff, Mr. Pitkeathly."

"Oh, thanks. I'd forgotten I left it here." He accepted the Oaken Staff that had been in the family for generations and allowed the porter to help him into his coat and charged after his new tutor.

As Kilbride trotted down the steps to the Underground, Pitkeathly noticed he wore trainers not shoes. He glanced down at his handmade shoes, comfortable without even being worn in.

Kilbride strode straight for the ticket gates and produced a travel card from his wallet.

"Sir!" Pitkeathly waved a hand at the machines. "Sir, I've got to buy a ticket."

Kilbride frowned. "Not got a travel card? What was Collier thinking of, making you pay each time? Hardly a proper use of allowances."

"He travelled by car, sir."

"I didn't know he worked exclusively outside London." Kilbride folded his arms and leant on the gate. "Hurry up, lad."

Pitkeathly sprinted over to the machines without mentioning Collier had used his car even in London. After all the College's cars were exempt from congestion charge. To Mr. Kilbride that was probably more improper use of privileges. He bought an all-day travel pass, not knowing where he was going, and made a note to send his man out for a monthly travel card later.

They emerged in one of the poorer parts of London. Collier never brought him along on jaunts like this. It was new already.

The jeans and shirt Mr. Kilbride wore, while cleaner than the ones around here, didn't stand out like Pitkeathly's handmade suit. He walked a little closer to his tutor.

They arrived at a frozen food store. A closed sign hung on the door.

"Right," Mr. Kilbride tapped on the door. "Background for you. This shop has seen a number of disturbances and the local vicar requested an assessment. Is it supernatural or the local kids?"

The door opened and a black woman peered out. "You the exorcists Father Cooper sent for?"

"That's right, Edward Kilbride and assistant."

She hugged the edge of the door as she studied them. "Didn't know the Church of England believed in that stuff."

"Not all of us follow modern ways. May we at least inspect the problem?" Kilbride said.

"Adyam Shebly." She stood back and opened the door. "Father Cooper told me you'd be okay. You'd tell me whether it's ghosts or kids."

Kilbride stepped into the shop and took in his surroundings. Pitkeathly couldn't feel him using any working.

"Perhaps if we—"

"Shut up for now, lad." Kilbride focused on the woman. "Have the 'hauntings' been tied to a specific spot?"

Pitkeathly was stunned. Mr. Collier always asked his opinion. This was no way to learn.

Adyam waved her arms about. "They're all over the shop."

"Who works here?" Kilbride asked.

"There's only me and my son, now," the woman said. "Can't afford staff with the drop off in custom."

"That would be the young man lurking behind the 'staff only' door?"

Pitkeathly stared at the door, but he saw nothing."

"Dauggie!" the woman shouted.

The doors opened and a mixed race young man emerged, his trousers hanging almost to his knees and beanie hat over his hair.

"Hitch up your trousers, Dauggie. This is Mr. Kilbride who is the man Father Cooper sent for."

Mr. Kilbride nodded. "I'll need a bit of space to work in—"

"So we don't get to watch." Dauggie turned to his mother. "Told you they was a fraud. Make sure you check 'em for goods when they leave saying the 'this house is clean' bit."

"—so if you could sit here at the tills to give me enough room."

The shop owner settled in a chair, but her son stormed away. "I'm not watching you fakers fool my mum. Adele says we are wasting our time on a food shop when we could be earning millions."

"I am not running a gambling shop," the owner said. "No matter what advice your bleach blonde girlfriend gives."

"It's not gambling." He slammed a fist into one of the freezer cabinets; the door swung open. "Just high end money games machines."

He batted at the swinging door to shut it and stalked towards them. Behind him the door failed to catch and swung open again.

"Now look what you've done," Adyam said. "You know I can't afford to repair any more damage!"

Fog glided out of the open door. It pooled on the clean linoleum and built into a column. It loomed over Dauggie.

The temperature in the shop plummeted.

Adyam jumped to her feet and her scream emerged as a cloud. "It's an Ice Ghost!"

Dauggie spun as the mist column toppled over him. He dropped to the floor like a board. The icy mist hung around and dripped on the floor.

"If you'd done a general detection as I was about to suggest—" Pitkeathly said.

"The freezer cabinets are Earthed, any working would transfer to ground, wasting power. Do you know nothing, lad?" Kilbride said,

Out of his pocket he pulled a wand. *"Purified seven times in the fire.* Get the son, you idiot!" He darted forward shouting over his shoulder.

The rise in temperature in the freezer center made the freezing fog melt faster. Pitkeathly raced to the fallen youth under cover of the heat spell. He hooked his hands under Dauggie's shoulders and made to haul him out of the puddle. His handmade shoes skidded on the slippery linoleum. He landed splat next to Dauggie, his fine wool suit soaked.

The mist retreated from Kilbride until it hung next to the open freezer door. Adyam ran up and grabbed her son, towing him out of the danger zone. Pitkeathly scrambled to his feet as Kilbride advanced up the freezer aisle.

In the -20°C air by the open cabinet the mist solidified again. This time it concentrated on forming a hand. It yanked open a second door, lowering the temperature, then a third. The creature began to take human form. Not just human it took man shape—for some reason the creature had genitals.

"Oh that's all we need," Kilbride said. "A yeti. *They are like the chaff, which the wind scattereth away."*

The shop door blew open and a howling gale slammed into Pitkeathly's back. He grabbed the handle of the nearest cabinet and clung on.

The mist thinned. The solid hand grabbed for the next freezer cabinet door and jumped inside flinging out packets of frozen food to make space. It slid along behind the door.

With an abrupt gesture, Kilbride cancelled the wind and stalked along the cabinets, flinging them open and peering in.

The yeti, now fully formed, jumped out of the end door. On slippery, ice feet it tottered towards Kilbride, opening the doors as it came.

The air temperature tumbled again, not just from the open doors. Kilbride hugged his coat around him and whispered a working— his breath drifted like smoke. Pitkeathly shivered in his wet suit.

The creature stalked towards Kilbride, lowering the temperature with every step. Kilbride hunched over as if the cold air was a punch in the stomach. Under his hat the tips of his ears were blue and his mouth was frozen, unable to even whisper the words of a prayer.

Pitkeathly backed away. A tutor taken down by a creature, there was no way a student of the college could take on such a monster.

"Get out there and do something, the man's getting hypothermia." Adyam shoved him towards the cabinet then ducked down under the till counter.

What was *he* supposed to do? He was the trainee. His tutor shouldn't get into messes like this. But then, he had rescued Mr. Collier from the well. Adyam was right, he had to do something. With the added bonus, if he freed Mr. Kilbride from this mess then his place at the College was assured.

What was he able to do?

Fishing Mr. Collier out of the well had been a matter of throwing down a rope.

What had Mr. Collier taught him? Nothing about yetis.

Mr. Kilbride dropped to his knees on the icy floor. The yeti opened its arms wide as if it was going to hug him.

Darting glances around, Pitkeathly snatched a bag of frozen peas which had fallen out of the freezer cabinet. He yanked it open with his teeth.

"*Thou hast broken the teeth of the Ungodly!*" He flung the bag of peas down the aisle.

In the arctic temperatures caused by the yeti, the peas froze into marbles. The yeti stepped on the rolling balls, skidded along the floor and landed in the puddle that had soaked Pitkeathly.

The liquid froze around the creature, pinning it down.

Kilbride uncurled his fingers and pointed the wand. His teeth chattered. "*Upon the Ungodly he shall rain snares and fire!*"

Loops of fire formed in the air as Kilbride circled the wand. They dropped onto the struggling yeti and held it on the floor as the air filled with steam.

From another pocket he produced a jar which he tossed at Pitkeathly.

He opened the jar and set it on the floor.

"Check the freezer cabinet where it first emerged. I expect the summoning spell is set in there."

"What should I expect to find?"

"If you can't locate something like that after two years in the college then you're a waste of space," Kilbride said.

Pride had Pitkeathly wafting away the steam from the melting creature and prodding through the bags of frozen vegetables. And there it was: nothing subtle about this one. It was a ... shaped ... ice cube, but he was reluctant to grasp it.

"Come on, lad, don't take all day."

Pitkeathly pinched the tip of the ice ... cube and lifted it into sight, holding it at arm's length.

Kilbride sniggered as he saw the elongated ice sculpture. "So that's why the yeti was 'male'. I saw similar novelty ice cubes advertised for hen nights in a catalogue. Drop it in the jar, lad."

The ice jingled against the glass. Pitkeathly rubbed his hand off on his damp trousers.

With another flick of his wand, Kilbride said. *"He shall take me out of many waters."*

The steam gathered into a cloud which drifted into the jar. Pitkeathly crouched next to it, melted yeti dripping from his fine handmade clothes. When all the steam was inside he slammed the lid on and screwed it down.

"For a minute there I thought I was going have to do all this myself. You've got a lot to learn, lad," Kilbride said.

Pitkeathly's mouth dropped open. "You weren't in any danger? It was a test?"

"All your training is a test. Maybe tomorrow you might want to wear more casual clothes. Leave the suits for Church on Sunday. Let's get back to the college and deal with that water elemental, hey?"

"We're not going after this 'Adele'?"

"And what proof do we have that she set the ice, er, novelty in the freezer? None." Kilbride pulled out his wallet. "Mrs. Shebly, I owe you for a bag of frozen peas and to get your floor cleaned. I've scorched it. Sorry about that."

Pitkeathly watched his new tutor pay for damages. These people owed him for clearing the demon and he was paying for damages. This was crazy.

Mr. Kilbride hadn't been in danger, he had been told to find out if Pitkeathly was any use. The trainee gritted his teeth trying to swallow the anger that burnt inside of him.

It was all a test.

He wanted to throw the jar on the floor and break it. Let them clear up the mess after that. The yeti was a weak elemental but teaching it how to take out a Witch-Finder was not impossible. He lifted the jar.

Adyam cradled her son's head while phoning for an ambulance. Her son was breathing, but unconscious.

Kilbride stared at the raised jar.

"It was all a test?" Pitkeathly demanded. "What about my performance reports? Aren't they good enough for you? My Uncle on the High Council thinks I'm good."

"What do High Council members know? They are shuttled up there from mediocre careers. It's rare that a good Witch-Finder ends up on the Council. We either die in office or retire to the least magic place we can find and shudder as we try to live normal lives. Today was not bad, but not the best performance from a second year. You need to work a lot harder than those reports from Collier suggest you do. So which do you want to be? An uninspired jobsworth, or a real asset to the College." He walked out of the shop. As he opened the door the howling siren of an ambulance closed on the scene.

His Uncle was a member of the High Council, but one of the strongest Witch-Finders in the College dismissed him as a 'jobsworth' like all the High Council.

Pitkeathly gritted his teeth. He wanted to be a dragon slayer—he did not want to be the one who set the dragon on the unsuspecting village.

He slipped the jar into his pocket and followed Mr. Kilbride.

Rekindle the Fire

The heat from the fire behind Gillian tickled her back.

-he needs your help, crackled the hearth, as she sat on the padded fender waiting out the current dance at her sister's New Year's Ball.

Gillian glanced in the direction the Fire Lady indicated. Alasdair and his Cousin Malcolm slid out of the ballroom while no one else in the room even saw the huge paneled doors open and shut.

With all the candles and open fires in the ballroom at Caisteal an Dunkley, the Fire Lady watched everyone—even though Gillian was the only follower in the room. Maybe the nature spirit had a perverse crush on the Alasdair Dunkley, a Church of England Witch-Finder. The red-headed Malcolm would be a more appropriate crush than black-haired, Alasdair.

Checking that no one—for instance her sister, Sylvia—paid any attention to her, Gillian drifted over to the door and out, to pursue the two men.

The paneled corridors of the Caisteal muffled their footsteps. Gillian crept after them.

Once away from the ballroom they strode into the back hallways associated with the servants. Here the carpets and paneling were replaced by bare wood floors and painted plaster walls.

They stopped in the hall by the back door. Gillian skulked closer, though her party dress and shoes made that difficult the lighting was dim enough. She leaned against the wall, paint flaking off and settling on her dress like massive flakes of dandruff as she tried to hear what they said.

Of course, they were speaking in Scots Gaelic. Gillian grimaced; with no flames out here the Fire Lady was not an active presence, so no translation.

From the inflection Alasdair had asked a question.

Malcolm huffed, and then answered him in another rapid exchange with a gesture towards the back door. Gillian caught one word: 'Sylvia'.

Alasdair sounded a bit put out as he answered.

Gillian had heard enough. It was up to her to sort out the messes Sylvia caused. She slipped away through the labyrinthine corridors of the Caisteal. Having found a staircase, she trotted up to her bedroom. Less than ten minutes later she was out of her party frock and in sensible outdoor clothes. Carrying her boots she made her way to the top of the back stairs.

Malcom had left but Alasdair sat, changing from his dress gillies to hiking boots. She wasn't going to have to track him down.

Unlike her, he hadn't bothered to change his clothes. He had thrown an Inverness cape over his dress tartan. He stomped his boots to settle them and then lifted a heavy spear from a display near the door.

As she trotted down the dark stairs, Gillian heard the ballroom orchestra striking up another waltz.

"Well, goodness me! Has Laird Alasdair found other amusements?"

Dunkley's hand clenched around the spear as he eyed her up and down. "And that isn't the pretty party dress you were wearing not ten minutes ago."

Gillian shrugged. "You've been so rude to my sister this week; please think how the servants and the rest of the clan will act when the favored heir leaves her first party early. So why are you the heir, not my sister's husband?"

"My cousin Malcolm makes a better Laird than I ever could since my father died in prison. I hope Douglas will follow Malcolm. I've no desire to step into my father's shoes." Alasdair's lips twisted as if he'd got a mouthful of crab apples. "The clan doesn't need another Black Dunkley as Laird."

Up here in his homeland, the Scots gravel in his accent was marked. Gillian tried not to let his voice caress her ears; she was Alasdair's friend, nothing more.

"Still, it would reflect better on Sylvia if you returned to the party," Gillian said. "Tell me what the problem is: I will solve it. That's the job of older sisters."

"No one will miss me. I'll be there at midnight when she sets off her New Year fireworks." He tilted his head to listen to the waltz. "Though I have to say on most New Year's Eves we'd a'be dancing eightsome reels five parts drunk on good whisky by now."

"I was right; the party isn't to your liking. You've found something else to do?"

Alasdair leaned on the spear. "Right! I've always had the bad manners to walk out on my cousins' plans when they bore me."

"So why the spear and all dressed for a walk in the snow? It's not a fancy dress ball; I talked my sister out of that."

"For which you have my undying gratitude." She saw the glint of a smile in his grim face. "I have reasons for leaving right now. As I said, I will be back for midnight. Perhaps you can save me the last dance?"

"Give me a good reason and I'll leave you to it. I can follow you—any working you put on me, the Fire Lady will remove. If she notices we're missing, my sister will accept you and me going off for a quick shag." She wanted to shock him into telling her what problem Sylvia had caused this time.

Alasdair winced. "No one would think there was anything like that between us. I've convinced everyone up here I'm gay, so they won't want me as their Laird Dunkley."

"Oh, so that's why the maid who brings up my tea on a morning is making huge hints about a wedding and trying to get my confidence? I want an explanation. Is it the Kooshee thing? I doubt the young men would talk about something soft and cuddly."

Alasdair leaned his head on the spear. "If I kill the *Cù Sìth* before midnight on New Year's Eve it will stay dead once and for all. And no more young men of the clan will go ahunting for the treasure and get killed."

Gillian frowned. "Is Douglas hunting treasure for Sylvia? No amount would be enough for her."

Alasdair kept his mouth shut.

She strolled over to where the coats were hung. "So what is a *Cù Sìth* when it's at home? What sort of treasure? Will I need to get a team in?"

"Archaeologist!" He scratched at his beard as he thought. "The best translation would be 'fairy dog'. Sometimes they steal women and bairns for the fairy folk, but other times they guard the dead ways and treasure—but fairy gold is not worth dying for."

"Okay, let's go." She hauled on a ski jacket.

Alasdair stared at her. "It's not your business."

"It's always my business to sort out the mess Sylvia leaves behind. She can't help being twelve years my junior and a shock to my parents."

Alasdair ignored her comment. "And how did you notice me leave the ballroom anyway? I've left behind a strong working such that people know they've just seen me. I won't be missed, I assure you."

Gillian grinned. "The Fire Lady gave me a kick when she saw you leave. She expects me to sort this out."

His eyes widened. "Is that so? I never thought of her as an ally. In that cupboard there are waterproofs. You'll need them in the snow—it's a fair hike up the Dun." He leaned his spear against the door and vanished down a side passage.

Well, that had been easy; she should have mentioned the Fire Lady earlier in the conversation. Gillian watched the door swing shut behind him. Oh well, he'd said she could join him so she rummaged in the tall cupboard to find waterproof trousers. She sat on the stairs to pull on some warm socks and her boots before kitting up for the weather outside. She knew it had stopped snowing but the wind still wuthered in the chimneys.

The door to the side passage opened and Alasdair returned carrying a candle lantern with the candle alight. He handed that to her and inspected the spear display again. Sometimes it irked her Alasdair knew more about Cræft than she, a member of a coven, did. Witch-Finders! She shook her head, mildly amused at her anger. The warmth of the Fire Lady covered her.

He chose a spear off the wall. "Do you know how to use one of these?"

She shook her head.

"You thump the shaft into the ground and brace it against your foot, like this." He demonstrated. "Then you drop the pointy bit towards your enemy and let him run onto it. The bar across the end stops the enemy from running all the way down the spear."

Gillian accepted the heavy spear. "I'm to carry this?"

"Is it too much? I left all my wolf spears behind and the iron blade will help against a Cù Sìth. A boar spear is the best protection I can offer you. They're huge dogs, bigger than Ross and Rory."

At their names, Alasdair's two wolfhounds poked their heads out of a nearby room.

"I'll give it a go," Gillian said.

He picked up his boar spear. "Come on boys, we have work."

They sniffed in disgust as he opened the door and snow drifted in on the high winds.

Gillian checked the candle lantern, the flame still burned despite the wind. She lowered the tip of her boar spear to get it out of the door and followed Alasdair and his dogs into the night.

Despite the moonless night and the broken cloud cover, the snow glowed with a fairy light under the few visible stars. The candlelight and the torch Alasdair picked up from a whatnot that stood beside the door cast enough light to see by.

The dogs, resigned to a walk in the cold, bounded away and chased the snow which blew into drifts against all the walls and trees. Gillian fell in beside Alasdair. Their footsteps creaked in the unmarked snow.

He carried the spear resting over one shoulder the base resting in his hand. She tried lifting hers that way instead of letting it drag in the snow; it lightened the load for a little while.

"So how's the recruiting going?" she asked. The drifting snow damped her voice into a whisper.

"As badly as ever." He shook his head. "The High Council insists we keep to the same old families even though a trawl through the general population finds gems like my apprentice. The 'virtue' as they like to call it runs low in the regular families."

"But so many of the older Witch-Finders are burning out," Gillian said. "I mean, extrapolating from what you've said and how exhausted you are all the time. How are they going to manage when a whole generation retires?"

"I don't know," he said. "When Josh takes over from me I foresee massive clashes with the High Council."

She forced her next question to be casual. "When will that be?"

"When the bastards get me," Alasdair said. "I'm resigned to dying on the job, far better death than going like Nathaniel. God keep us all from that. I should have known it was serious, not burn out. He's my friend."

With her hands full, she rubbed her arm alongside his. "I am sorry about him."

"Just having someone I can talk to about my work, like I used to with Nathaniel, helps keep me sane. Thank you, Gillian."

"And a witch-friend even knows what you're talking about." She had to change the subject away from his dying. "So how is it possible you managed to skip being Laird Dunkley after your father died?"

He shrugged. "I work for the Church of England. Guess who the head of that is and the source of all these silly titles. Getting the change to the collateral line made permanent was impossible, though I tried. They believe I'll want to take up the post after I retire—I never will."

Okay, another subject to avoid, what else? Oh yes, coven news. "We're about ready to bind that minor air elemental you brought to the coven. The secondary circle we built over the summer is consecrated. Ellen wants to bind it on the balance day."

"I'm interested in watching that ceremony." He accepted the change of subject. "I'm surprised no one else has ever tried to change an elemental from evil to good by worshiping it in a different way."

"You stunned Thomas and Ellen when they got the research grants." Gillian giggled.

"You'd never believe what grants people have left in their wills, and the ones pertaining to the supernatural we have the discretion to award." He studied the ground pointing out the footprints the wind hadn't blown snow over. "Well we know someone came up here, it's not a wild goose chase. Douglas is too impulsive—it's a trait of all the Red Dunkleys."

"You said you were a Black Dunkley, what did you mean?"

He took the lead now. "Red hair and black hair for the most part, but the reality is, Red Dunkleys are warriors, and if a *Cù Sìth* could be killed by swords or guns, then there'd be none left in the Highlands."

"And the Black Dunkleys?"

"We're all sorcerers." He shuddered, but she knew it wasn't the cold, like her he controlled his body temperature with magic—even if he refused to call it magic.

"You mean your father …?"

"He controlled my mother with magic, yes. She'd never have stayed with a man like him without the spells. I didn't know better until I met Nathaniel Trewithick. By dragging me into the College, he saved me from the same life as my father."

"Oh that's why you refuse to call what you do 'magic'."

"It really is Practical Theology." He flicked a glance at her. "You might want to petition your Fire Lady for some protections, we're nearly at the Dun." He hesitated a moment then added, "I'll have to bring you up here in the summer—it's a vitrified fort."

"Oh goodness! I'll bring my tools." She glared at him. "I bet you even know how they are made?"

"Maybe." He gestured his playing dogs to heel.

Gillian lifted the lantern. Inside the candle flame took shape as a small woman.

-Of course I've got protections around you, ask for more help when you need it.

Alasdair leapt through the snow. A body lay on the ground. She stumbled after him.

Gillian heard Alasdair whisper, "Màiri!" as he dropped to his knees beside the young man. Gillian set down her candle lantern and grabbed up the torch to give Alasdair light to work.

He sagged as he pressed his fingers to the young man's throat. The man was her brother-in-law Douglas Dunkley. That explained Alasdair calling out to Douglas's mother, Màiri. Was Sylvia a widow?

Alasdair's shoulders relaxed. "He's still alive. Luck of fools."

Wisps of steam arose around Dunkley's kilt as he worked to help Douglas, his magic or Practical Theology kept his bare knees warm as he knelt in the snow next to the cousin. He leaned across and smelled his cousin's face. "Drunk too, though how he managed that on the fizzy pop your sister was serving, I don't know."

"That was best champagne!" Gillian had been shocked when Sylvia told her the price per bottle.

"Aye, but it wasn't good whisky." He reached into his Inverness cape and brought out a silver packet that he unfolded. Of course, Alasdair would have a survival blanket on him.

Gillian held the torch on Douglas as Alasdair rolled his cousin in a cocoon of silver.

Darkness crept over the snow at the edges of the circle of light, which was odd now she thought of it. The snowfield had been clear for miles when they were walking up here.

She squinted into the dark. "Ross, is there something out there?" She pointed as she called the dog's name. Ross jumped to his feet and sniffed around in the snow.

Alasdair saw his dog on the task as he continued with lifesaving measures for his drunken cousin.

Ross growled, low.

Ice that had nothing to do with the cold weather settled on her chest. Fear stole her breath but still she lowered the spear point.

"Alasdair, is a *Cù Sìth* a green dog about the size of a bull?" Her voice came out as a squeak as the huge creature edged forward, like a cat stalking a bird.

Rory sprinted to his brother's side between the humans and the creature, feet set, growling low and threatening.

Alasdair jumped to his feet with the spear in his hands and joined the dogs. "Ross, ceart. Rory, cearr."

The dogs split up and circled, left and right.

"Gillian, stay back. Help if there's a way but stay safe." He kept his eyes on the creature. Advancing, he kept his spear point low.

The *Cù Sìth* backed away to keep all three of the main opponents in view. Ross and Rory followed it, creeping low to the ground.

"*Show us the light of thy countenance.*" Alasdair called out, the blowing snow hushing his usual ringing tones.

The darkness that had hidden the approach of the *Cù Sìth* fled. Gillian watched it draining into pockets in the rocks and skulking behind trees: it was a living darkness.

Without its darkness, the *Cù Sìth* raced away, further into the Dun. Gillian set Alasdair's torch down near the candle lantern holding the presence of the Fire Lady.

Ross and Rory waited for Alasdair, and then they ran in a closed formation after the creature.

Not being a fool, Gillian turned this way and that, to make sure the creature didn't circle round to get to the easier prey: the man on the ground and herself.

Douglas groaned as she twitched the survival blanket tighter around him. She clenched her gloved hands around the spear shaft. With the darkness banished, the whole vitrified fort was visible. They called the forts Duns around here. This was the Dun of the Kleys. Gillian grinned.

She heard Alasdair shout something. Snow absorbed the sound, but he faced away from her and the words had a sharp, magical edge to them so she assumed it was directed at the creature rather than her.

The *Cù Sìth* pounced on Ross.

Gillian prepared to run and help when she saw Rory snap at the creature's black Mohawk of a mane. As the creature twisted to attack Rory, Ross jumped up and bit the creature's leg.

Alasdair circled and rammed his spear at the *Cù Sìth*.

It dodged and shook off the dogs, hurtling away.

Again Ross and Rory kept in a group with Alasdair. This was the first time she had watched them working together. The work Alasdair put into training his dogs impressed her. If one ever got lured away from the protection of the other two they would be in danger.

Now she'd lost sight of the *Cù Sìth*. She darted glances around and saw nothing but the darkness as it crept out again.

"Could you do something about that," Gillian asked the candle lantern.

-you need to learn more respectful prayers—like your Alasdair does with his God. Choose more burnable locations for battling demons in the future: this time snow, last time pouring with rain.

"Please?"

The candle flared and darkness slid back into its hiding spaces, more tightly hidden than before, exposing the Cù Sìth as it stalked easy prey. Gillian stood between downed Douglas and the creature. She lowered the spear point. It circled round her.

Again, ice closed off her lungs.

"Fire Lady, I beg…" she gasped.

Warmth filled her. *-Maybe I was joking about the respect. Get the request out.*

Ross and Rory bounded through the snow, with Alasdair close behind. Their silence was spooky.

"The bloody thing won't stay still to be bound." He'd raced through the snow to her side and he wasn't even panting. He advanced with his dogs.

The creature ignored him. It fixated on the candle lantern. It had noticed the Fire Lady.

"Kill it!" Gillian shifted position to get the candle lantern behind her.

"What? Kill a nature elemental in front of *her*?" He concentrated on the *Cù Sìth*.

"What?" Gillian stared at him.

"Oh for heaven's sake, joke," he said. "I have to bind the bloody thing to get it to stand still long enough to skewer it."

The creature circled to get at the Fire Lady.

"*Thy lightnings shone upon the ground!*" Alasdair pointed his spear at the *Cù Sìth* and lightning spurted from the end.

The creature dodged and came in from the other side. Gillian turned: for some reason it hated the Fire Lady.

"I'd forgotten about that," Alasdair said. "I should have insisted you and the Fire Lady stayed behind."

"What?" Gillian said.

-Tell the idiot I can protect myself from such a creature.

Gillian relayed the information, but Alasdair shook his head. "I'm not talking about the *Cù Sìth*. I've got to finish this and get you all out of here."

He glanced down at his cousin Douglas then flung the spear to the ground. He yanked at his plait and pulled out a long strand of his hair.

"*The Highest gave out his thunder, hailstones and coals of fire.*" With his toe he drew a circle and the snow inside the circle melted. "*The springs of the waters were seen.*"

In front of him, he now had a little pond. He took the strand of hair and wove it through his fingers.

"I bind you to me by the contract with my ancestors," he shouted. This time the hills echoed with his words—though he was speaking in Scots Gaelic, the Fire Lady translated them for Gillian.

Alasdair raised his arms above his head. His aura filled with black. The dark shadow, which the Fire Lady had chased away, crawled out of its holes and from behind trees. It crept along the ground not towards the *Cù Sìth* but towards Alasdair. His eyes were black holes in his face.

Gillian shrank away from him, crouched near the candle. It was the only light and warmth in the area. Even the stars blackened out of the sky, perhaps the clouds had returned, but it didn't feel like it.

This wasn't Alasdair Dunkley. Not the one she knew. Ross and Rory growled: threatening.

-*Stop him! He mustn't do this. You must keep him away from his darkness.*

The panic in the Fire Lady's voice forced Gillian to her feet. She wanted to stay huddled in the only light available.

The *Cù Sìth* set a reluctant paw forwards, moving towards Alasdair.

Ross and Rory bared their teeth at him.

"Stop right now!" Gillian said.

So lost in his actions there was no indication he heard her. Gillian took two steps and slapped his face.

"Stop! Look at your dogs!"

His black, blank eyes faced her without seeing. "How dare you!"

Gillian slapped his face again and stepped back between Ross and Rory. "Look at your dogs!"

They growled, standing on either side of her prepared to leap at Alasdair's throat.

"Ross, Rory what are you doing? *Thugainn thu.*" He pointed at heel.

The bared their fangs, setting their feet ready to attack.

"Why have your dogs turned against you?" Gillian demanded.

He stared at his hands. The black aura coruscated around him. The darkness in his eyes faded. He dropped to his knees. "What am I doing? *Wash me thoroughly from my wickedness and cleanse me from my sin. For I acknowledge my faults and my sin is ever before me.*"

Gillian watched the dark aura drain away. Unlike the other darkness, it didn't slink into hollows in the ground—it drained into his soul, where she had seen a black core of him when they had worked together last time. He buried his head in his hands and whispered something to his dogs in Scots Gaelic.

The *Cù Sìth* barked. The noise rolled around the Dun like thunder—worse even than the deafening roar of fighter jets flying in low practice flights. Gillian slammed her hands over her ears.

Alasdair buried his head in his hands. Released from the control he had exerted over it, the creature barreled towards them.

Her body still quivering with the roar from the fairy dog, Gillian snatched up the nearest boar spear. She thumped it on the ground and braced her whole body for impact.

Ross and Rory ran to her aid. They darted in from the sides herding it towards the spear.

Unable to move from its path it tried to slow, but at the size of a bull its inertia was too great.

"Stop being a Drama Queen! Help me!" she shouted.

Alasdair dropped his hands and pushed to his feet but his boots slipped on the slushy snow around his knees. Herded by Ross and Rory, the creature ran onto the spear point.

The impact shuddered through Gillian. It jarred her shoulders but it was hold the spear or die. The creature writhed on the impaling blade as she strained to remain on her feet.

It howled and the sky called back with more thunder. The noise rattled her whole body and her heart skipped in irregular beats. She wanted to drop the spear and block her ears. Another bark from the *Cù Sìth* would be unbearable.

"Burn!" Gillian gasped.

The Fire Lady's power burst through Gillian. It ran up the spear shaft straight into the creature's face. Fire stole the oxygen, strangling the third call of the *Cù Sìth*. Steam rose around the creature until it became a vapor drifting around the end of her spear. Then it was freezing mist blown by the wind. The shaft of the spear crumbled into black powder and the iron spear head thudded to the snow.

The Fire Lady burned brighter than she had ever done before.

"NO!" Alasdair clambered to his feet. "Not here. Call her back!"

The Fire Lady danced up into the sky.

"What's happening? It's better than fireworks." The delight of the Fire Lady at being in this place filled Gillian. In the lantern the candle guttered and died. "What's wrong? She likes it here."

"This place is affecting her. They vitrified the walls of the Dun by worshiping a fire elemental into a frenzy. The *Cù Sìth* is a water elemental; it killed them when they burnt low. Call her back."

The Fire Lady danced around the Dun. The snow melted as she burned brighter and brighter. Under her feet the dormant grass flared up and burned down. The peaty soil below the charred blades began to smolder. Overheated rocks cracked and pinged as they melted.

Gillian snatched up the lantern. She wished Thomas or Ellen was here; the elders of the coven had more authority with the Fire Lady. "That's enough. You need to get back into the lantern.

-Weeeee! This is marvelous. I've never had so much strength and this is memories of worship. You will have to find out how they did it here.

"Come back to the lantern," Gillian shouted. The Fire Lady's song of joy drowned out the call.

"Listen to your worshiper." Alasdair raised his arms again. "*Speak through the Earthquake, wind and fire, voice of calm!*" His voice echoed over the Dun with the strength of his years of practice with this Practical Theology—given the black sorcery he had performed she knew the difference now.

"Come back here and sit in the lantern, please." Gillian held up the candle lantern.

"Thrice it is said. And binding," Alasdair said.

The candle flame re-ignited. *-What do you want? I have power to dance with.*

Alasdair slammed the door shut. He snatched up a handful of pure snow. Before the Fire Lady burst out of the lantern he traced the sign of the cross over the door of the lantern, then all the sides and the cap. "*The ungodly are trapped.*"

"What?" Gillian pulled the lantern away from him and reached for the latch. Inside the Fire Lady screamed and pounded against the glass.

"Take her down." Alasdair heaved Douglas over his shoulder. "If the Fire Lady is to survive this night, take her out of here before you open that door."

Should she trust him? He had used black sorcery. It was the dogs that swayed her. They slunk towards Alasdair, as if they had been Bad Dogs.

"I'm sorry, boys. You were right to warn me." With one hand balancing Douglas, he bent to scratch their ears.

Gillian raced down the path, following their upward track. Half way down, the Fire Lady stopped pounding on the glass sides. She stood in her candle flame with her head bowed as flaming tears rolled down her cheeks. Well, that was Gillian out of the coven, but she kept the lantern shut until she reached the Caisteal.

Alasdair pulled open the door into the back hall. "This way. I can arrange it so she is none the worse for her imprisonment."

He led them to a pantry which stored strong spirits. He tipped Douglas on the floor and grabbed a bottle of whisky.

"Stand aside." He set the lantern on the floor opened the bottle. He tipped it over the candle lantern as he opened the door. And sprung back.

The Fire Lady burnt larger than life, consuming the alcohol. Flames scorched the walls of the pantry. She wagged a flaming finger at Dunkley's nose. Gillian smelled singed beard hair.

-Do you know how many of my kind were sacrificed to make that fortress?

"Eight," Alasdair said. "Eight of you were destroyed to build a secure home for the clan in a fierce world. Tonight it was nearly nine. For that I am sorry, as you came to help me."

The Fire Lady turned her back on him and stared at Gillian. -*Thank you for getting me out of there.*

"I'm sorry I had to trick you," Gillian said. "I didn't mean to. I thought he intended to persuade you."

-I was not open to reason, and he knew it because he knows the spells. He set them off when he tried to bind the creature by the clan callings. The Fire Lady swung round on Dunkley, her fiery finger scorching his nose. -*Get me more spirit. I'm weak from your binding.*

"I'll give it to you outside," Alasdair said. "The house is inflammable."

He grabbed the nearest bottle. Gillian winced as she tried guessing the price of it, but Alasdair didn't even notice. She followed him out of the pantry carrying the Fire Lady in her lantern, with the door left open.

At the back door, Alasdair opened the bottle and set it on the back step, sheltered from the wind and the snow. The Fire Lady hoped from her candle and settled into a small flame burning the whisky.

-This is good stuff.

Alasdair shut the door on the tipsy nature spirit. He leaned his forehead on the doorframe. "I am not a Drama Queen. I regularly have to wrestle with ... that side of my nature."

And now he was being pompous. "If we added mud," Gillian said, "we could charge to watch the wrestling match."

He glared at her.

"Though I daresay someone as rich as you doesn't need to charge."

His anger was replaced by puzzlement. He crouched and tickled his dogs' ears. "What makes you say that?"

"Handing a bottle of best Scotch to the Fire Lady to burn—she'd have been as happy with a bottle of meths."

He laughed. "There's no best Scotch in that pantry. The best stuff is locked in the cellar."

He rummaged in a cupboard. He tossed her a towel and knelt to dry Rory. "I'm not a drama queen, am I?"

"Sometimes you are over melodramatic." She dropped into a crouch next to Ross and toweled his damp fur. "When did you learn black sorcery?"

"In my cradle. I wasn't dramatizing when I told you Nathaniel saved me. Once he joined the College, he knew he had to convert me or fight me. I find it difficult to resist temptation."

"Well, let me add a bet on the outcome of that wrestling match." She got nose to nose with him. "If I catch you using black sorcery again, I'll skin you alive and feed you to your dogs."

"Fair enough." Alasdair checked his watch. "You might want to run up and get into your party dress before anyone decides that we're off having a ... ah ... that we're in bed together."

He hung up his Inverness cape and settled on a bench to change from his hiking boots to his gillies.

From the pantry, Gillian heard a wail and shriek from Sylvia. She must have found her missing husband, drunk and in a puddle of whisky. Gillian fled—at least he was still alive.

What's the Magic Word?

Mike fiddled with the York Tourist Information Centre map. He twisted it upside down, as if he were a lost tourist, and then glanced around as if trying to find a street name plate. Of course he knew where he was, but he checked out the name plate on the covered snickleway—Whipmawhopmagate—and peered at the map as if trying to locate this name in the maze of streets printed on the page.

"What are you doing, Dad?"

Mike's hiking stick dropped to the pavement with a clatter. He spun around. An eight-year-old boy stood in the entrance to the snickleway, with his coat over his pajamas and wearing trainers without socks. Mike raised his eyes heavenwards, praying for patience before he spoke.

"Timmy! What the … I mean what are you doing here? You're supposed to be in bed."

Timmy rammed his hands in his coat pockets and glared at Mike. "Mum's putting Trudy to bed, so I followed you. I wanted to make sure you're not sneaking out every night to cheat on Mum."

"I'm at my job. Your mother knows all about it, but now I have to walk you home." Mike crumpled the map in an angry fist and thrust it into his coat pocket. "And your mother would prefer it if you called me Mike or Uncle Mike."

"You're married to Mum. Anyone can have you as an Uncle. I want a Dad."

Mike winced. "It's not as if I mind what you call me, Timmy. But top of my to-do list is keeping your mother happy. So let's get you home and—"

"Why would anyone put a skull mask on a dog?"

Mike scooped up his hiking stick and spun around. "What?"

A huge black dog with glowing red eyes, and a face—as Timmy had noted—like a skull crept down the covered path towards him. The creature sprung.

Pointing the spike of his hiking stick at the dog Mike shouted, *"He cast forth lightning and destroyed them."*

Lightning sparked from the metal point and flung the dog back down the passageway. Its claws scrabbled on the stone paving slabs. Not waiting to assess the damage, Mike grabbed Timmy's hand and hauled him out onto the main street. No one else was around.

"You're a wizard!" Timmy said.

"Run, Timmy!" Mike glanced over his shoulder and saw the black dog racing after them. He yanked on Timmy's arm as the boy tried to watch the dog.

"What is it?" Timmy shouted as he dragged on Mike's arm trying to see the creature.

"It's a Barghest!" Mike caught Timmy in his arms and sprinted into Colliergate. Watching his step he raced towards King's Square and the modern street lights.

"It's gone," Timmy said as they passed Barnitts.

Panting, Mike set Timmy down on the raised cemetery section of the square that in summer the street performers used as a stage. "You could have got us both killed by following me."

"Can you teach me to be a wizard?"

"Sally would kill me," Mike said. "I'm taking you home."

"Were you hunting the bar guest?"

Mike settled on the platform next to him. "I was trying to get it to hunt me. But yes, I'm a wizard and my job is to keep Yorkshire clear of dangerous creatures like the Barghest."

"Why was it wearing a collar?"

"How should ... hold on a minute, the Barghest wore a collar?" Mike glanced around the Square to make sure the creature wasn't creeping up on them again. They were in the clear, but still alone. That made Mike suspicious; it wasn't late.

He checked his watch, it was only nine o'clock. Any number of tourists and University students should be out sampling the night life, but it was silent for streets around.

"*The firmament shall show his handiwork,*" Mike said.

"What are you doing?"

"Hush, Timmy." Mike stared around at the empty streets with his other Sight. He saw gossamer gates across the streets, each one distracting the people with the idea that somewhere else would be better. As he inspected the spider webs of light he thought about going for a coffee. He stood, breaking his link to the spell.

No, he had to find out how to cut through the magic gate. He tried looking again, but his mind drifted onto other thoughts the moment he examined them.

He broke with the spell again.

"Dad," Timmy said. "What are you doing?"

"I'm trying to find a way out of here, so I can take you home."

"Can't we stay out for a bit longer? It's not like there's any school tomorrow."

Mike was unsure how long it would take to break through one of those gates, but he had to try. He couldn't get into a fight with a monster while protecting his wife's son. Timmy's presence made tonight's Barghest hunt a waste of time. There might even be tourists caught in this Barghest trap and he would have to leave to take a small boy home.

Mike tightened his grip on his hiking stick. He mustn't blame Timmy for this. He should have known a boy would be curious. He should have set spells to stop Timmy from following. It wasn't Timmy's fault this night was a failure. If he told himself that enough times he should believe it.

"Let's get you home, hey?" Mike said.

Mike clasped Timmy by the hand and walked towards the nearest invisible barrier. It was at the end of the Shambles. Timmy dragged on his hand.

"Can I have some sweets?"

Mike viewed the sweet shop. Within moments, Timmy dragged him along to show him the poster of a comic book.

Words whispered in his head. *You don't want to go this way. There's pizza along this road. The boy will like the Fudge Shop on Low Petergate.*

It was hard to resist the magic in the words, it was so subtle.

Mike shook his head to clear it from the misdirection spell. "Timmy, this way now."

"But I don't want to go home." Timmy dragged on Mike's hand. "My friends get to stay out late."

"Your mother will be worried."

"You'll take care of me."

Mike yanked on Timmy's hand and pulled him close to pick him up. "We're going home now."

Timmy kicked him, but Mike tightened his grip. *"Oh send out thy light and thy truth, that they may lead me."*

He saw a gap in the spell.

"Are you doing more magic?" Timmy gasped in awe.

"Yes, I'm trying to take the spell off you."

"There's a spell on me?" The boy examined his hands. "How can you tell?"

"Because you're stopping me from taking you home."

"It's far too early for bed."

Following his lead for a break in the gate spell, Mike sashayed between two metal bollards and swung into another covered snickleway, this time towards the market. The black dog lunged into the other end. The image of escape vanished. It had been a lure.

The dog advanced up the snickleway.

Mike deposited Timmy and raised his hiking stick. *"My bones are smitten asunder as with a sword."*

He brought the stick down in a swipe as if he was using a sword.

The black dog flinched at the blow that hit its shoulder. It recovered and leapt straight for Mike.

He dived out of the snickleway.

Timmy stood right in the path of Barghest.

Cold horror hit Mike. He had forgotten Timmy for a second. In that second he saw Sally weeping over Timmy's grave. He trembled as she blamed him—but her accusations were always less than he blamed himself.

He lifted a hand but dread stole the magic words he needed.

Timmy scooted to one side. The creature hit a metal bollard with a musical clang and recoiled dazed. In a flash, Timmy slipped the collar over the dog's head. He held it up with a pleased grin.

"Here, Dad."

Air whooshed into where the wolf-sized Barghest had been and now a dazed Yorkshire Terrier sat rubbing its nose on a paw and whining. Mike examined the collar. It had '*fidelis usque ad mortem*' stamped on it.

It wasn't dead, but who was the dog supposed to be faithful to?

"Fide… whats… it? A dog like this shouldn't be called Fido. He's a Rover." Timmy knelt down and stroked the dog. "I saw the collar, you didn't. I helped you defeat the bad dog."

The dog sank its belly to the ground and whimpered when Timmy said those words. Its coat was black and matted, with a patch of white over the forehead. It pawed a Timmy's knee. Timmy patted the dog's head, before Mike caught his hand.

"There, you can be a good dog now," Timmy said. "He needs some dinner."

A man staggered around into the covered walkway from the market end. He leaned against the wall. His face was white with spell backlash, but he saw the dog and pulled himself upright.

"You interfering little brat." The man pointed a wand at Timmy. *"In eius locum substitui."*

A black dog shaped cloud ran towards Timmy.

Mike slid in front of Timmy shouting, *"Arise and help us and deliver us for thy mercy's sake."*

The spell which would have substituted Timmy for the dog slammed against Mike's counter spell and evaporated. Mike jumped to his feet.

"Not you again." The warlock glared at Mike and lifted his wand.

"You dare attack him!" Mike shook his hiking stick as if it was a Viking spear. "You dare say magic words to harm my son!"

The warlock shuffled back, driven by Mike's rage. The man had crossed wands with Mike over his rain and flooding spells last week.

"Can we talk about this?" the warlock said. "I didn't know he was yours."

"Well, now you do." Mike pointed the spiked end of his hiking stick.

"Get him, Dad."

"Thou makest us to be rebuked of our neighbors, to be laughed at and scorned, and had in derision of them around us!"

The warlock glanced left and right, then backed away. He lifted his wand, but the force of Mike's words shattered the bone it was made of. His eyes rolled back in his head and he collapsed to the stone paving slabs.

Mike heard shouts from the market. He gathered up Timmy and the dog and whisked them out of the snickleway as people arrived.

"He's drunk—even this early."

"Call an ambulance, someone."

"Why bother, prop him against the wall and let him sleep it off."

Mike carried Timmy out of hearing. His son—it didn't matter what Sally said. Timmy was his son.

"Come on, Rover," Timmy shouted over Mike's shoulder. The dog trotted after them.

With the warlock unconscious, the barriers had dissolved and Mike set Timmy down on the pavement. "We'll drop that dog off at the RSPCA, but I'd better phone Sally. She'll be frantic by now." He slid out his mobile phone.

"Can't we keep him, Dad?" Timmy hugged the ragged Yorkshire Terrier.

Mike lowered the phone. "Like he's going to get on with your mother's cat."

Two sets of puppy dog eyes pleaded with him. "Please."

Not even Mike could resist that Magic Word.

Listen to the Beasts

This is how it starts.

It's late. Darkness washes up to the cones of light around the streetlamps. Your company is your shadow that lengthens and circles as you move from light island to light island. It darts up side streets, and then re-joins you as walk alongside the next office block.

From the way you stumble down this city street, I guess you've been drinking. Traffic growls along the North Circular, a siren howls, but close by the only sound is the clump of your shoes on paving slabs. A ringing rattle, you spin in a terrified circle. The night breeze rolls an empty bottle along the gutter. With a hand on your heart, you slow your panting breaths.

Why are you here? Maybe, you're lost. There's not even a pub nearby. Cafés that served the workers in daytime are closed. The workers in the loading bays have long since departed. Lorries joined the slow traffic out of London. The gates are barred and night watchmen make their rounds with snarling dogs.

Behind you, the street light crackles out. In front, the light fizzles. The night breeze whispers between the darkened sweat-shops.

Do you hear the foot fall behind you? Almost in time with your own. Sometimes in step, sometimes a beat out.

That's me. I'm your protection.

You'll never notice me. By day, I'm like you. I have a job, a respectable one. But now, it's after hours.

That's when the Night Creatures hunt.

You check behind you.

But I'm not there. There's a set to your shoulders that suggests you're going to peek. I've learned that well. I'm always close to a hiding place. This time I duck into a doorway. Another time, I will slip over a wall or down some steps. Shadows assimilate me.

Reassured, you walk on.

You don't notice the woman. She wears a power red suit. By day she's a stock broker, revved up the adrenaline of the floor. Buy, sell;

she can make or lose millions. All that stress requires special energy. After work she goes for a drink with the 'boys', a prayer to her God for a successful hunt. At night, she feeds on sex. You'll believe she's a prostitute, right up until the moment she tears your throat out in her frenzy. She's a maenad, if you want her proper name. You get all sorts of immigrants here. Me? I'm a native.

She recognizes me and steps away from you. You are not her prey.

The clump of my clogs matches your footfall. It's an echo from the way the factories and vacant offices loom over you. You try to convince yourself, but ragged heartbeats drown out your reason. There's a pulse in your throat. It makes you sick with terror.

Behind you a white-scaled, clawed arm lifts a manhole cover. I take care to tramp it down.

The creature under the cover howls like an ambulance siren in the distance.

For your information, that's not an urban fox rummaging through the commercial bins. It's a familiar from the local Black Coven: I recognize the beast. In a city like London you get a mix of cultures. They bring their beliefs with them. A fox around here could as easily be a Finnish Firefox, or a Japanese Kitsune.

It raises its hackles, but backs away. It respects me.

You jump at every little noise now. I'm sure your mother, or if not her your grandmother, warned you about walking alone at night. Did you ignore them because this is the modern, non-credulous world? And you can take on any human mugger, right? Think again. You see, this little island on the Edge—Europe or the Atlantic take your pick—is a playground for those who belong in the Night. And you are their toys.

The fear streaming off you is almost orgasmic.

Yes, there are far worse things than me out there, but they acknowledge my priority. I got here first. I match my heartbeat to yours and feed.

At least I won't kill you.

The fox raises its head, sniffing the air. It bolts.

Alert, I extend my senses. "No not they! Not now!" Surely it's not that time of the month already.

I'm sorry; I know it's never polite to leave in the middle of dinner. My feet take off without conscious decision.

The shout goes up behind me. "It's Gladders. We've got him this time."

Of course, there are those who appointed themselves as your guardians. They call themselves Church Inspectors; we of the Night call them *Witch-Finders*.

As I glance over my shoulder, I clog dance on the manhole cover. There are three of them on my tail.

The manhole cover clangs open. A white, toothy snout peeks out. "I'll get you boggle!"

Where there's belief, a spirit will feed and take shape. I hurry on. I hear his squeal as his hatch rumbles shut over his lair. The clang again. One of my pursuers has pried open the cover. He drops into the sewer.

One down, two to go.

With a breaking heart, I ditch the clogs. They are part of me. They induce fear. They help me feed. But I can't flee for my life in them.

The concrete is hard under my bare feet. Stones and broken glass are there to rip my soles. Hard road jars my joints with every step.

I tear down a side street. Their heavy boots pound on the pavement behind me. Touching the street poles as I pass, I shut out the lights. I scurry left.

They're still behind me, inexorable. In my induced darkness, I sprint to the next corner. I must lose them. I'm not a killer. Why do they bother with me?

All around the industrial estate I hear cries. One night in the month, the Witch-Finders train their recruits on us Lesser Creatures of the Night. The whole pack of them must be out tonight.

The shouts are louder now. I flatten against a wall. My breath hisses as I try to still my heart. Two members of the local Black Coven make a stand against three of the young Witch-Finders. The warlocks are dressed in silly black silk dressing gowns; their opponents wear sensible jeans. Magic flickers the scene.

I can't stay here. My pursuers' boots sound close. The warlocks hold the other lot. I appeal to my spirit. The lights in the main street flash out. I race across the road. More side streets beckon.

My throat is raw from panting as I run, but there's no water here.

The warlocks take advantage of my dark. They are gone by the time one of the baby Witch-Finders reignites the street lights. A halloo and they gallop away; the hunt is on again.

I force my aching body to run faster. Getting clear of this pack of predators is first priority.

"There! There's Gladders."

Damn! Not again! I scramble away and two men charge after.

Up ahead, I sense more fear. While running, I cannot feed, but I know someone who can. I angle my flight that way.

"Pitkeathly, cut him off."

Do they think I don't understand them? Once I was human too, before I embraced the Night.

There was a girl, a lady. She made my heart pound the way my feet pound now.

Back in the 30s, we were at University. I was the first in my family to enter University. A farm boy made good. She—what was her name now? I can't remember anymore—anyway she was from money. Slumming it, her friends giggled about our relationship, but I know she loved me. She wanted ... odd things. But I loved her so I went along with it.

The Night swallowed her and I was unable to rescue her. A Vampire spirit took her: no one intervened. I tried to fight it off with the Light, I tried to save her and bring her back to Christ. But the servants of Christ—these Witch-Finders—murdered her.

I wandered long in the pain of my loss. How to protect others like her? To stop them from accepting the Darkness into their hearts.

And then I had my epiphany: make them remember the fear of the dark, the way all humans used to. I accepted the spirit of a boggle into my soul. Its previous carrier was already dying. All I did was help him end his misery.

I am not a killer, all I do is make you scared. I want to make you so terrified of the Dark and the Night you will no longer place yourself as prey for those who live in the Night.

I am your protection. Why do Witch-Finders hound me? I'm trying to make their job easier.

Down this alley. I hear them howling in exultation. They are like beasts themselves on this hunt. This is dead end. To them.

"Analay! He's trapped!"

The Maenad is feeding here. The younger pursuer stops; his mouth drops open in lust. He staggers towards her vision of perfect beauty. He pushes aside the first victim. The rejected man claws at my pursuer. The Witch-Finder swipes him with his stick.

I leap over the spiked fence. The iron in the railings is agonizing, like ice as it burns my hands, but a fox will chew off its own foot to escape a trap. Landing, I slip. My foot catches in a pot hole. The spirit in me forces me on; pain shoots up my leg. Beyond this fence is waste ground.

I risk a glance behind me. The other man, Analay stops. He must rescue his comrade. He punches the Maenad—a first! A gentleman hit a lady? Unheard of. Her nose gushes blood. The two victims turn on Analay.

I stagger on. The Witch-Finder-lings hunt in a pack, others might lie in wait. Iron in the fence would trap most of my compatriots of the Dark. I have to hope they stationed no one in this rubble and straggly grass.

The pain in my foot eases as the spirit directs attention from fleeing the threat to keeping the body alive. I run, until I hear no more noise.

The wasteland ends in a housing estate. Barefoot and limping, I walk through the empty streets. Clogs are hard to find these days. I'll have to search the internet again; I can't use the same supplier twice. It will alert the hunters.

Once the leaders were Carr and Trewithick. Then came Marishes and Dunkley. Now the beaters shout Analay and Pitkeathly. You have such short lives.

I was born in 1908. One day the boggle that possesses me will wear out this body and move on.

Until then you are safe. I protect you from those far worse than me.

Dawn creeps up through the clouds. I haven't hunted tonight. Maybe I'm walking down your street now.

I'm starving.

Red Hair and Gold

Ducking into a passageway, Josh flattened against the wall.

"I would have hid myself against him." He gathered essence of Tudor brickwork and timber framework around him like a cloak.

A figure pushed a clanking wheelbarrow across the end. He ignored the covered alley and the person hiding within.

Josh sagged. *Phew, that was close.*

Creeping to the entry, Josh peered through the encroaching dusk, checking up and down the cobbled street. Monsters of his imagination lurked in every shadowy alcove. With no lights, the overhanging levels of the ancient houses changed the street into an inky abyss.

When he had wandered through the York tourist hot spots earlier today, this street stank—if you had a nose trained to detect the stench of evil. The street, which locals called The Shambles, was an old butcher's market; its cobbles, soaked in blood for over a thousand years, made it a perfect place to summon monsters.

Seeing no one, Josh slipped a hand into his jacket pocket and drew out his torch. It clattered against his knuckledusters. Taking a chance, Josh flashed the light along the cobbles to check that the City Council hadn't planted a bollard anywhere about here.

The light caught on a newssheet; black lettering shouted:

Copper Thieves Target Electricity Substation!

Josh glanced up—that explained the unlit streetlights.

A scrape behind him. He twisted, lifting his torch. The cosh aimed for the back of his head hit his ear and neck. The pain drove him to his knees as he warded off a second blow.

It struck his arm.

He dropped the torch and groped for his knuckledusters. The third wallop from the cosh flattened him. His nose crushed against the cold cobbles.

He clung to consciousness as hands, under his arms, dragged him along. The man huffed as he hauled Josh's dead weight over the top of the wheelbarrow.

Retaining enough wits, Josh stayed still—no attempt had been made to restrain him with the coils of wire he lay across.

The barrow was too small to carry his length so his toes scuffed the ground. The barrow weaved and swayed through Newgate Market; Josh saw the empty stalls looming out of the dark.

They stopped briefly and foul smelling air wafted out of an opening door. The attacker picked up the handles and pushed Josh into the men's toilets on Silver Street.

A low voice chanted. "Jabez Wilson. Jabez Wilson. Jabez Wilson."

Josh was tipped off the barrow—he managed to roll face up and squinted around. His attacker picked up a battery lantern and studied him.

By that light, Josh saw another man standing over a table set with an open book, a wine bottle, and some chocolates in scarlet wrappers.

"Your spell worked!" the attacker said. "It's a red-headed man!"

The muttering stopped. The chanter set his wand on the table. "You doubted me, Ryan?"

"No! Not at all!" Ryan stepped back holding up his hands. "I'd never doubt you, Sid."

Sid glowered at Ryan. "Address me as Magus!"

"Yes. Sorry. Magus." Ryan scuttled to replace the lantern.

The foul air in the toilets, mingled with the earlier scent of evil, acted like smelling salts on Josh. Through lidded eyes he studied the rest of the set up. Copper wire trailed over the edge of the barrow. Sid Magus had smashed a toilet, which accounted for the worse than usual stench in the men's bogs. Beside the broken ceramic sat a drugged-out chicken in a cardboard box—no, it was a cockerel. Underneath the cockerel ...

Josh scrambled to his feet. "Do you have an archbishop's license to experiment with basilisks? Though I have to say, substituting sewer methane for the usual volcanic hydrogen sulfide was inspired."

His captors stared at him. Almost choking on the stench, Josh strode over to the broken waste pipe. "Shoo!"

The cockerel blinked at him. Josh clapped his hands and the bird staggered to its feet. Underneath the bird was indeed a toad's egg. Josh produced a plastic shopping bag and a disposable glove from his pocket.

"What're you thinking? You can't create basilisks in a built up area without a grade three alchemy laboratory and a containment structure of a Solomon's seal or above. As per Defra regulations."

"Regulations?" Sid struck a pose. "What are you talking about? I alone have rediscovered the Ancient Arts of Alchemy and Magic. I have immersed myself in the-"

"Sorry to break in on your Evil Monologue, but as a Church Inspector of Cræft users, I've heard it all before." Josh picked up the egg with a gloved hand and placed it in the shopping bag. Dropping the glove in after, he tied the handles. "I know people who run correspondence courses about this stuff."

Ryan perked up. "Really?"

"Oh yeah, plenty of covens—"

"Dabblers!" Sid hissed, snatching his wand up from the cluttered table. He raised it above his head in a dueler's pose. "*Causa Mortis*..."

"*Braccae tuae aperiuntur.*" Josh dug his hand into his other trouser pocket.

Sid frowned as he mouthed the words. Josh belted him one on the chin with his knuckledusters. Sid slid down a cubicle divider, dropping his wand.

Josh smirked. "I said, 'Your flies are undone'."

Ryan sidled towards the door as the wand rolled towards Josh. Scooping it up, Josh turned to Ryan. "Look at this! He's not even trying. What self-respecting Master of the Dark Arts uses a *cow* thigh bone for his wand?" Josh snapped the wand over his knee and dropped the pieces to the floor.

"No!" Sid screamed. He raised his hand. "*Ignis-*"

"Not in here, y'prat!" Josh swept up the docile cockerel and sprinted for the door. Ryan took a second to grab Sid's book from the table and followed.

A damp blast blew them out of the toilet door. Smoke roiled out behind them.

"Of course, magic is dangerous." Josh jumped to his feet. "That's why you need Inspectors."

The lights left on for security in the local shops showed a convention of confused, red-haired men milling around, as a scorched Sid crawled out of the smoke-filled toilets.

Josh snatched Sid's book from Ryan's hand. It fell open at:

On turning base metal Copper into Gold.
Mix the blood of a red-haired man with ashes of a basilisk ...

A Poltergeist Love

Pitkeathly watched Analay as he sprawled in a leather armchair to read the letter. He would have given anything to know what Mr. Dunkley was telling Analay.

Analay scowled at Pitkeathly. "What t'hell does Mr. Dunkley expect me to do with you for two weeks? Oh sit down for God's sake or I'll need a telescope to talk to you. If you can sit in those painted-on jeans."

Pitkeathly flopped into the chair opposite Analay. They were in a corner of the senior students' common room for sixth and seventh year apprentices. Pitkeathly had never been in here before. The lounge room was littered with newspapers, wands, athames, and staves. A drinks bar took up one corner. He drank in air smelling of incense, worn leather and good whisky.

"I go where I'm told." Pitkeathly ran a finger over the fine leather arm of his chair. He wanted a part of this room. "It's not like I earned the privilege to tell my seniors what to do."

Analay flung the letter to one side. It joined a pile of paper on the floor, writing side down.

"So what do you want to do?" Analay asked. "Mr. Dunkley insists we have things we can learn from each other."

Pitkeathly scratched at his head—unlike the other Witch-Finders he couldn't bring himself to grow the ponytail. Analay wore his ginger mop in a long plait, but that was the privilege of the Watcher and his apprentice. Pitkeathly was proud of his looks, though less so now after a year of working with Mr. Kilbride.

"I don't know, sir."

"Quit that right now, I'm Josh. Actually, do you have a girl friend?"

"I beg your pardon?"

"No, seriously Ken, do you?"

"I prefer Pitkeathly to Kenelm."

"Who wouldn't? But Ken's not bad—he's a super handsome boyfriend of Barbie, and it so happens I have an idea along those lines."

"Cut to the chase, An … Josh?"

"Can do. We have too many sisters and female cousins ending up in the 'Recovery Centre'. You wouldn't want your sister Fenella to end up there would you?"

Pitkeathly heard the quotation marks around 'Recovery Centre', justified in his opinion—no one 'recovered' enough to leave. But … "What do you know about my sister?"

"Huh? Come on, you know it's part of my duties to assess possible candidates for the College?"

"Girls can't join us!" Pitkeathly sat bolt upright, hands clench on the chair arms.

"Have you watched the way she charges up the pitch with her hockey stick, to the detriment of her opposite number's shins? It terrifies me. Imagine her wielding a wolf spear, true Valkyrie material there."

"She wants to be a games mistress."

"I rest my case. You know what saves the College from a gender discrimination lawsuit? We don't exist."

Pitkeathly's fists curled. He wanted to slam a right hook into Analay's plebby face for even mentioning his sister.

Analay leaned back in his chair and hooked an arm over the head rest. He grinned at Pitkeathly, a challenge to do his worst. Pitkeathly wasn't stupid; Analay was one of the best the College had ever trained. He relaxed his hands.

Analay's eyes crinkled in amusement. "So I want to set up a dating agency between the College members and the various female relatives."

Pitkeathly shuffled in his seat. "We're not allowed to have regular girlfriends."

"And Mr. Kilbride has gone to Tenerife with some random woman and her kids, right? Name me one of the older guys who don't have a steady girlfriend."

Pitkeathly grinned. "Mr. Marishes."

Josh snorted. "Okay, you got me there. There's no drama queen like an old queen when he's convinced he's a perv. Mr. Dunkley has a regular spiel that talks sense into him and back to his boyfriend … sorry, gentleman friend."

"What about Mr. Dunkley?"

Josh tapped a finger across his lips. "Mr. Dunkley campaigns for changes to our rules on marriage. I've no idea if it's for a personal reason."

"Not that you'd tell me, anyway," Pitkeathly said.

Josh winked at him. "But, back to my plan. I have no idea how dating agencies work. You're tall, dark, handsome and posh; women will fall over themselves to date you. Sacrifice heart and soul for the College, that sort of thing. Find a terminal, set up a few profiles and see how it goes. Report back next week, if you can find me." Analay picked up another folder. "I've got to check out unexplained arsons in Milton Keynes every Midsummer's Day for the past three years. It's Midsummer on Friday."

***

As far as duties went, this was one of the more pleasant. Here he was assigned to help a sixth year while his tutor had a holiday and instead of chasing the usual lot of monsters he was having dinner dates, lunch dates, dates in a wine bar and now he was waiting in the coffee bar at Euston Station for another date to arrive before heading off to the theatre. In between social activities he was trying to work out the computer algorithms for the matches. A nice rest, but he would be ready to go back to normal when Mr. Kilbride returned.

His alert triggered—the one he used as a warning when a demon was stalking him—and he looked around for his date. A woman walked in the door and waved to him. She must have memorized his profile picture. She strode across on power heels, wearing an above the knee skirt.

Ever the gentleman, Pitkeathly stood to greet her. "Ellia, let me get you a coffee."

She dropped her bag on the table. A sensible one, which jarred with the power heels—it had an outside pocket for an umbrella.

"That's okay, Ken. I'll get one while I'm on my feet." She cast a glance over the table as she flipped open her bag and retrieved her purse.

He winced inside as she trotted off, but kept the welcome on his face and settled back on his high stool. He had learned on the first date you had to let women share the cost of a date if they insisted.

She appeared at the table carrying two cups. "I saw you'd nearly finished yours. My train wasn't that late."

"Oh no!" Pitkeathly pushed aside his half-finished cup and accepted the fresh. "I came here straight from work—the tube trains were running on schedule so my estimated travel time decreased."

"You don't say on your profile what you do." Ellia perched on the stool opposite and crossed her legs: long and lean.

He dragged his gaze away from knees covered in sheer, black nylon. "I test computer games." That was the easiest thing to say, so if he mentioned killing a demon he claimed it was in a game. Pitkeathly sipped the fresh cup of coffee; from her quick glance at the table she had guessed what type he enjoyed. He took another mouthful.

"And that pays well?" She eyed his suit.

He glanced down at his suit to make sure the Savile Row label was hidden. "For some reason, people pay me so I can destroy their games. I'm not complaining."

"I prefer logic puzzles to shoot 'em ups. How about you?"

"It depends on my mood, but I get a great deal of satisfaction from gunning down a demon."

"How so?" She cradled her coffee as if warming hands, despite it being Midsummer's Eve. "A spell or a sword would be more appropriate for a demon slayer."

They chatted about magic systems in the latest releases until the coffee shop overheated. He ran a finger over his collar to loosen his tie. He drained the dregs of his coffee, and finding his hand trembling he set the cup down carefully.

"I ..." He blinked as his focus wavered.

"Don't you worry," Ellia said. "I know what to do. You're so perfect: intelligent, handsome."

"Thank you, I think." He let her raise him to his feet.

Come on." She tucked a hand under his arm and led him out of the coffee shop. "This train is on time."

"Train? Aren't we going to the theatre?" He had to obey her. "Have you put a spell on me?"

"Gosh no!" She laughed at him in delight. "Magic is in the games we were talking about, silly. I have a little task for you. If you're a little off, that would be the Liquid E I poured into your coffee."

Magic he'd talked about magic, what was he supposed to say to counter that, oh yes. "I test computer games."

"Yes, we agreed they were fun." She helped him onto the train and into a seat. "Stay there."

He knew he ought to move but you know it was easier to do what he was told so he smiled at her.

He jerked awake. He shouldn't be sitting on a train.

But he wasn't, he stood against a wall with his arms outstretched. His head ached. He tugged on his arms, but chains held him in place. Glancing down, he flushed—she had removed his clothes. But she had him standing on a thick, rubber mat. Was that to insulate him from ground—if she believed he practiced magic—or was it to keep his feet from freezing on the concrete floor? Either way it was good for him. The room smelled of fresh paint.

"Are you with me yet?"

He saw Ellia dressed in a white lab coat. In fact the whole room had a laboratory style to it. White walls and standing over to one side was a white lab bench with metal stools. A metal mushroom stood in the center of the room. Pitkeathly recognized it from school—the smaller version from school science lessons generated static electricity that made your hair stand on end. What this larger creation was going to do had him worried. Between him and the mushroom, two metal poles were driven into the concrete. Equidistant from each pole stood a pile of dirt as if a mole had dug through the floor. To one side Ellia had stacked her winter wood pile. What the hell did this signify?

She had mentioned working for a pharmaceutical company, but this was more Frankenstein than drugs research.

"If you'd told me you were into S&M, I have a friend who would like to meet you."

Ellia laughed, not a mad scientist cackle but a pleasant chuckle. "It's nothing like that. Let me explain."

"Please do." As long as she was monologueing he had a chance of getting out of here. "Any chance of my coat? It's a bit cold, you understand."

She checked a clock. "Not yet. It will be dawn shortly and that's when I run my experiment. I need the heat boost from when the first rays of the Midsummer sun run down Midsummer Boulevard and hit the mirrored surface of the station."

"Experiment?"

"I've had such a bad experience with men I've decide to make the perfect boyfriend."

"So where do I come in?" Frankenstein and all that came to mind. He needed to be out of here. He tugged against the cuffs holding him in place against the wall.

"Please don't damage your body; I need it to remain perfect. I have discovered a way of creating an electrical intelligence and I need to induce it to create the perfect body to go with it."

"A golem?" Pitkeathly asked, interested in spite of his uncomfortable position.

"That implies a slave rather than a real human," she said. "I've got you chained up there so it has a blueprint to work from. You're safe from any discharge on the rubber mat. I've tried this every midsummer for the past three years and for some reason the electrical intelligence has refused to build the body. It must be the chosen blue print is imperfect but you—"

An alarm sounded. "Time to get going. The sun is rising. When the sun strikes the mirrored surface of the railway station, I will create the electrical intelligence."

Panic stabbed his stomach. Keep her talking. "How does that happen?"

"I'll tell you later." She stared at her watch with a hand on a switch.

Oh well, now he had to try something he'd been told about. "Thank you for the explanation, but I don't want to stay for your party." He closed his eyes and prayed, please let this work. "*Let us break their bonds asunder and cast their cords away from us!*"

Desperation fed his prayer. The metal cuffs holding his wrists burst apart as she flipped the switch down. He gasped in relief. She stared as he stepped off the mat towards her.

"You can't do that!"

Static electricity lightning from the giant Van der Graaf generator arced to the two metal poles. From the poles two strands of lightning joined in a giant electrical 'Y' to earth in the pile of dirt on the floor. Pitkeathly smelled burning, then a ball of lightning bounced into the air. Ellia slammed a hand down on a second button and he witnessed the birth of a fire elemental. He lurched away from the creature.

It touched down on a pile of wood, which flared up around it.

"Now!" Ellia pointed at Pitkeathly. "Form a body like that one."

The fire elemental drew its flames into the figure of a burning man.

"It's working. It's working!" She held tightly clenched fists under her chin.

In work mode now, Pitkeathly saw her belief feeding the creature. The heat it generated scorched his skin. He eased away from the creature.

The movement attracted Ellia's attention. "Stay still. You'll make it all go wrong again."

The fireman lumbered towards Pitkeathly.

"The springs of waters were seen!" he shouted.

The creature flinched away—too young to resist the power even in his untrained voice. It circled the metal poles. Everywhere its fiery feet trod it left footprints of flame. Denied one victim, it stumbled towards Ellia.

Pitkeathly sprinted to the woman's side. *"Let them fall away like water that runneth apace."*

The creature flinched as drops of water condensed out of the air and fell on it. It snatched up a log from the woodpile that burst into flames in its hand. It chucked the burning missile at Ellia.

Pitkeathly grabbed her hand and raced towards the bench tugging her after him.

The burning log crashed onto the workbench and knocked a tin of paint onto the floor. It rolled along and settled next to the bench as he pulled Ellia down.

"No! Not again. It's all gone wrong," Ellia said.

"What the hell do you mean by 'again'?" he hissed. He grabbed the tin of paint and read the label.

"It's supposed to build a body after I induce the electrical intelligence. It's not supposed to be a poltergeist. But every year I have to repaint over the scorch marks from the last time."

Another burning log-missile thumped on the bench and skidded over the edge. Ellia kicked it away.

"Water-based, that's good." He jumped up and took in the contents of the bench. He grabbed a metal spatula and ducked back down. "The fire elemental is out of control because you don't believe in it."

Using the spatula, he levered up the lid of the paint tin.

"What are you doing?"

"I'm trying to work out a way to distract the creature while I run for your fire extinguisher. You should keep it closer than by the door."

"What are the words you are saying that makes it run from you?"

"Magic." He lifted the lid. "Trouble is, I'm only in my third year at College. I'm not supposed to practice without a licensed Official nearby."

"There are Further Education courses on Magic?"

"Oh yes, and we are always meeting up with folks like you—re-inventing the wheel."

He peered out from their safe haven. The creature sat on the burning woodpile, replenishing its flame.

The creature staggered to its feet and plodded towards the bench. It left little burning footprints, which sputtered out with nothing to burn on the concrete floor.

"You expect me to me to believe in 'magic'? I am a scientist! I don't 'believe' in something without proof."

He hefted the tin of paint to get the weight. "So why do you carry an umbrella, even though it's midsummer and hasn't rained for two weeks?"

"I beg your pardon?"

"We all know if you forget your umbrella it will rain."

"That's different."

He smirked. "Of course it is. Stay down."

He jumped up from behind the bench and lobbed the paint at approaching fire elemental. An arc of white paint coated the elemental and it hissed and spat as the tin passed straight through it and clanged on the floor. Pitkeathly sprinted for the fire extinguisher at the main door.

The fiery man grabbed one of the stools around the lab bench. The metal was white hot in seconds.

Pitkeathly scrabbled at the catches on the fire extinguisher holder.

The outer door burst open. The heat from the fireman drew more oxygen into the room in a huge gust. It fanned the flames and the fireman grew. It threw the burning stool at the person who walked in the door.

"*I shall be whiter than snow.*" The chair cooled and clanged on the wall. Pitkeathly had never been so glad to see anyone, even Analay, who stalked towards the fireman ignoring the junior student. "*I am poured out like water! My body is even like melted wax!*"

The creature flowed down to the floor like a used up candle. It stretched out an arm, desperate to reach another log to feed on, but missed.

Pitkeathly fumbled the catches open and grabbed the fire extinguisher. He circled the edge of the room. Ellia peeked out from behind the bench.

"Wax!" Ellia shouted. "I should make a mannequin out of wax for next year—perhaps with all the elements for a human body."

Hearing a voice, Analay noticed Pitkeathly. Keeping his main focus on the fireman Analay said, "What t'hell are you doing here, kid? You're supposed to be doing the dating thing?"

Pitkeathly pointed at where Ellia sat cross-legged still sheltered by the bench scribbling on a notepad. "My date decided to use me to create that … that thing!"

Analay sniggered. "You are a bit sunburned—all over."

Pitkeathly gritted his teeth and armed the fire extinguisher. Aiming it at the fiery puddle of creature he shouted. "Get rid of it!"

The fire extinguishing foam covered the fire elemental and eased off the heat on Pitkeathly's bare skin.

"Oh yes. Sorry." Analay produced a glass jam jar containing a small amount of oil. Taking off the lid he set it on the floor. "*The Lord that ruleth the sea has a glorious voice.* Get in the jar."

The creature struggled and tried to flow towards Ellia, but Analay's will held it firm and it poured into the container. It found the oil and tried to flare up, but Analay slammed the lid on.

"Who are you two?" Ellia stood up from behind the bench, slipping the notebook into her lab coat pocket.

Analay stalked towards her. "We're Witch-Finders and look-ee here, we've found us a witch."

"Hold on a minute. I'm a respectable scientist. I created—"

"Josh, she's been creating fire elementals. Here in the lab!"

Analay stared around. "How?"

"She creates ball lightning and then believes in it …"

"I beg your pardon; it's nothing of the sort." Ellia strode out from behind the bench. "I use a proven method to spark the electrical intelligence by using an encephalograph. If you can monitor brain activity with the encephalograph then you can induce it to conform to the—"

"Show me the equipment," Analay said.

"This is my private—"

"Here," Pitkeathly said. "She uses the Van der Graaf generator to produce static which bursts out as ball lightning, and then this button must operate the encephalograph she's talking about."

"This is the first time the electrical intelligence decided to attack one of the men I wanted it to use as a blue print," Ellia said. "They others went wild and threw things round the lab. So I called the fire brigade and slipped the man some more Liquid E. While the fire brigade is putting out the fire, I dump the blueprint male. Men are so stupid; if you leave them chained to a bus stop wearing ladies underwear and a traffic cone, they're convinced they've had a good time—even if they can't remember it."

"I know what I saw and it was her belief that sparked the life in the potential. That's magic." Pitkeathly glared at Ellia.

"Now who said 'sufficiently advanced science' and all that," Ellia said. "How did you get out of the bindings?"

"Sufficiently advanced science," Pitkeathly said.

"Find your clothes, kid," Analay said.

"I have them here." Ellia opened a cupboard and dumped a pile of clothes on the bench. "And then you can get out. I need to plan my experiment for next year."

"No more experiments, madam," Analay said. "We're taking all this back to the college to study it."

Pitkeathly stared at all the equipment. "How on earth are we going to get it on the train?"

Analay pulled out his phone. "That's what we have fifth years for. They can bring a removals van."

"I'm only in my third year." Pitkeathly snatched up his clothes and turned his back to pull them on.

"You'd be surprised what you can get away with as Mr. Kilbride's apprentice."

"You're not taking my lab anywhere or I'm calling the police," Ellia said.

Analay slid his phone away unused and Ellia smirked. Analay grabbed her by the arm and twisted it behind her back. He had her wrists in cuffs before she squawked.

"Unlike Pitkeathly here, I'm not a gentleman." He twisted her arm more as he leaned forwards and whispered in her ear. "In this jurisdiction, we are the police. What part of Witch-Finder did you fail to understand? We are also Judge, Jury and ... Executioner."

"What!" Ellia wrenched her arms against the cuffs, but they held. They should: standard College equipment would hold a werewolf.

"Don't worry, Ellia." Pitkeathly tucked in his shirt. "We haven't intentionally burned anyone since the 1950s."

Even Roses Have Thorns

The taxi that brought Josh Analay onto the moorlands was already a mild echo in the gathering twilight. Everyone else up here had their cars pulled up against the dry stone wall, leaving passing room on this single track road. Mr. Dunkley spread out a map on the bonnet of someone's fancy Volkswagen.

Mr. Kilbride and Pitkeathly, his student, climbed over a stile set into the dry stone wall and strode away in the direction Mr. Dunkley had pointed. Karl Stempress and his brother Philip followed them but split off on the other side of the wall. Other tutors scattered to places pointed out on the map.

Josh approached, eyeing Ross and Rory, the huge wolfhounds who sat at Mr. Dunkley's feet alert for any danger. Ross, or maybe Rory, gave a little woof-let as a greeting and Mr. Dunkley set aside his map.

"I'm glad you've arrived," Mr. Dunkley said. "We're going to need you."

"Oh sure." Josh set his backpack on the ground. "What's the case, then?"

"There's another storm rolling in tonight," Dunkley said. "A number of the wind turbines have set alight over the last few weeks."

"Since you're here, I'm guessing it's not the high winds as reported." Josh examined the map. "What do you need me for?"

"The wind turbines are programmed to shut down when winds get too strong." Dunkley scratched at his beard. "I'm guessing at this point that magic is involved."

"And I'm the best at spotting magic flying around, huh?"

"If I've got a witch sniffer on the team I'm going to use him." Dunkley pointed to his map. "Let's get to this cairn. We'll have a good view of all the wind farms around here."

Josh studied the map assessing his tutor's judgment. He touched a block of gray that indicated buildings. "What are these? You ain't telling me people live out here."

"Urban fox." Dunkley flicked Josh's red plait. "However this time I expect you're right. I imagine they're ruined shepherd's crofts."

"Why bother putting ruins on the map?" Josh folded the map along the folds and handed it to his tutor. He eyed the rutted track up to the cairn and the gathering night with distaste.

"Here, you'll need this." Dunkley tossed him a miner's light to wear.

Josh fitted it over his head and then switched it on. As he shouldered his pack, Dunkley packed the map away.

"These things are going to alert everyone for miles around we're hunting them." Josh switched it off again and let his eyes readjust to the gloom.

"Let's get going."

The wind picked up as they hiked up the track. Each gust held the cold edge of rain, but nothing fell yet. Their waterproofs whisked with every step. Their boots squelched in the bogs from the successive storms. The dogs sprinted through the worst bits but they were still muddy and wet when they reached a drier trail.

The first rain fell. Driven by the wind it pounded on their waterproofs. Josh tugged the hood over his head. Dunkley reached inside his waterproof cape and brought out his phone. He reduced the light but the display still cut through their night sight as he read off the text.

He snorted. "Stempress senior is complaining about the peat bogs while Stempress junior has discovered the moor has gorse bushes," he reported.

"You need to stop sending Philip out wi' Karl. Philip resents his older brother being more powerful," Josh said. "And Karl tries not to be the elder brother so Philip isn't getting proper moral guidance."

"Truly?" Josh almost heard Mr. Dunkley taking a mental note. "So who would be the best senior to guide Philip in your opinion?"

"If it were me, I'd slide him out of t'College. He doesn't have the core of raw strength to be one of the Inner Circle and won't cope well with being of lower rank."

They chatted about College business until the rising wind meant they had to shout their responses.

On top of the hill nothing blocked the wind. They staggered into to the lee of the cairn and wiped off their faces. The wind whistled through the stones of the cairn and set the heather lashing around.

"You know, me Mam thinks I have a cushy life at Uni," Josh yelled. "I hope you're right about tonight, I don't want to be back up here for the next storm."

"It's my best guess," Dunkley shouted back. His dogs huddled at his feet. He hunkered down, sheltering his dogs under his Inverness Cape.

Josh slid down the cairn and set about unblocking his major ability. If he went about without the blinds down so to speak he would go mad. Many witch sniffers did. It wasn't a common ability, but most of the ones alive were in the pay of the other side.

Dunkley produced a thermos flask of tea and poured out two cups. Josh sipped his, cupping his hands about the plastic mug and relishing the warmth after the hike up here.

Josh sat bolt upright, spilling his tea over his waterproofs.

"What's the problem?" Dunkley set aside his drink.

"There's a wildfire wandering around down there." Josh pointed into the blackness.

Dunkley flicked on his head lamp, and produced his map and compass. "Any idea at distance?"

"I'm trying, but it's a different sort of plane."

Dunkley drew a line on the map. He found his mobile phone and tapped in a general message as Josh tried to get a better reading.

Flames fluttered in the darkness then the wind blew them out. The person tried again.

"There's an untrained and uncontrolled wizard, like us, at full power down there." Josh jumped to his feet. "Burns about the same strength as you or Trewithick."

Dunkley scrambled to his feet. He tipped out both cups and flung them into his pack. He switched off the head lamp.

"We need to get down there right now," Josh said.

Dunkley set a hand under Josh's elbow. "Lead us in the right direction. I'll keep us out of the marsh."

Josh was grateful for the hand steering him away from the worst patches of soggy ground: witch sniffer mode drowned out the real world. The dogs scouted the way ahead, guiding Dunkley around the budding lakes.

"To the right," Josh said. "He's moving away."

Dunkley halted them and checked his text messages. "Kilbride's in place to intercept them."

"Tell them to keep back," Josh said. "Whoever it is, is terrified."

"You see the emotions?" Dunkley's thumb flashed over the keypad relaying the instructions.

"There are panicked spurts of power."

"One person using power?" Dunkley asked. "Philip tells me he saw two."

"I may need to be closer. The one trying to set fire to the windmill is flaring too much. It's covering anyone nearby. They blocked out Philip's presence. He's too close."

The flare of power moved fast. Setting aside the panic, there was a familiar feeling to the power, but it wasn't anyone from the College. Josh recognized them as columns of light scattered around the moorland.

Dunkley sent out a frantic text. That flaring was getting too panicked. No time to wait for his tutor, Josh sped through the darkness.

His boots slipped in the wet grass and he skidded. Waving his arms around, he kept his balance, just. He had to slow down, but he had to pick up the pace. Whoever was below needed his help, urgently. He skittered a few more feet.

The wolfhounds raced ahead of him.

Ross batted against his left leg. Josh adjusted to the right. Just in time, his feet splashed in the edge of a pond. Ross put on a burst of speed as Rory directed him—in the dark he had no idea what he'd missed.

"I've got to reach that girl." Josh knew that was correct, the person using the power was female, and young.

Karl paced him. Up ahead the girl was staggering but being dragged.

"*His ears are open to their prayers,*" Josh muttered.

"Wolves!" a girl screamed. His spell caught the words and brought them to his ears.

"There aren't any wolves in England. Keep running. They'll take you away if they catch us." That was a man.

With that identification, Josh saw control spells running from the man to the girl. In her panicked state she kept throwing them off while he struggled to retain them.

Josh picked up the pace and tried to haul back on his Sight.

Philip ran in shouting, "*I will lay me down in peace and take my rest!*"

Alerted to how close the pursuit, the man dragged the girl faster. Josh cursed and sprinted after them.

"They've come for you Jade Rose, run," the man shouted. "Nearly safe."

Jade Rose's aura flared in panic. He was close enough.

"*They were brought in great fear where no fear was,*" Josh shouted, throwing the damping spell at her. He knew what was needed to calm the girl.

He raced after them.

Up ahead, the girl stopped. Her power levels dropping under the influence of Josh's spell.

Still half-seeing in the witch sniffer spectrum Josh watched the man's control spells reassert.

"Run, Jade Rose," the man ordered.

She tried to tug away, but she was too used to the control spells. She probably didn't even recognize they were in place. The man dragged her along at high speed.

"They stopped it. They can help me!" Jade Rose said.

"No one can help you except me," the man said. "Get us inside."

She pulled her arm out his grasp. "No they stopped the nastiness."

"Get us inside, now."

The girl fought the control spells and lost. Josh watched the girl working another spell. He charged after them and ran straight into a gorse bush.

He bit back his curses. He switched on his head lamp and caught Philip in the glare. "We ordered you to stay back. You can't expect your workings to influence that girl."

"I was in the right place," Philip yelled back.

Karl put a hand on Philip's shoulder. "They did tell you to keep back. No one wants you hurt."

Philip threw off the hand. "I don't know why I'm here at all. After all, I'm no use to anyone."

Dunkley and Kilbride walked up so Josh bit back further reprimand. He spun and stalked over to the gorse hedge. Under the light of his lamp, and the lamps of the others as they were switched on, he studied the unnatural growth. The bushes grew twisted and bent by the prevailing west wind, so much so natural, but the smallest spines on this gorse bush were 20cms long. The yellow banana-like flowers grew to hand size and the wind tore them into ragged lace.

He had one thing no one else here had. He had 'Seen' how the girl got through the hedge.

Josh lifted a hand and remembered what Jade Rose had done. *"He shall be like the tree planted at the waterside."*

Behind him he heard Kilbride and Karl Stempress reporting to Dunkley. He saw Kilbride's apprentice trotting around the hedge from the other side. His hearing spell was still in action.

"A man and his daughter, at least the girl calls him 'Da' so I expect they are related," Karl said. "He called her Jade Rose."

"Jade Rose! No!" Dunkley said. "Josh stop, you can't go in there alone."

Josh was part of the hedge. Dunkley tested the edge of the gorse thicket, attempting to wilt the gorse. Gorse traditionally protects against witches and Dunkley was the last person who'd be able to pass through, given his past.

"Has anyone got a machete?" Dunkley shouted.

Josh had no idea what upset Dunkley so much, but he had to reach the girl. It was almost a compulsion.

He emerged from the gorse hedge, and stumbled against a dry stone house. His head lamp picked out where new moss had been stuffed to block out drafts. It would have had a slate roof but someone had repaired it with corrugated iron sheets. The rain tapped out xylophone tunes on that roof.

He smelled smoke. He reached a corner and switched off his lamp. Light emerged through a window over which someone had nailed translucent plastic feed sacks to block the weather.

Josh crept to the window and tried to hear over the musical rain.

"I told you they'd come for you! Only I can protect you."

"Da, one of them stopped the nastiness," Jade Rose said. "It's gone away. I'll be able to go back to school. They won't call me mad anymore."

"When this storm gets worse, they'll go away, and we can take out another of those windmills. Can't have them building them this way, they'll knock down our home."

"Why won't you call me Rosie, like Mam did? Me Mam would want me at school."

He saw shadow figures as the man rushed across the room. The slap of flesh against flesh and the girl crying.

"Y'Mam left us.

Josh's damping spell was wearing off. The girl was angry. Josh ducked under the window and ran to the door.

He saw the flare of power. He kicked open the door. And stared straight at Jade Rose. He stopped dead.

"What t'hell?" Taking into account it was a pre-teen girl, he might have been facing a mirror. Oh, there was a slight oriental cast to her eyes, but the red hair flamed in the night.

She stared at Josh. The power drained away in shock. She jerked her gaze to her Da and back to Josh.

Josh turned to the man. If the image in a mirror aged, that was Josh in forty years. "You're in prison. Me mam would have told me if you'd got out."

"Joshua! Well, you've grown up posh and fine, haven't you?" Da eyed the expensive, and reliable, waterproofs.

Josh bit back the urge to reply they were provided by the College. He had to remind himself he had no need to explain his situation to this man.

Jade Rose clung to the camping kettle, as if it were a shield. "Who is he, Da?"

The man opened his mouth to speak, but Josh jumped in. "I'm Josh Analay."

"You were born Joshua Dilkes and that's who you are. Nothing *That Woman* can say will change it."

"S'not what me Mam says," Josh said. "It's what t'Judge says."

"You're my brother?" she whispered. He only heard her because of a lingering effect of the hearing spell he had used earlier.

"Judges," Da said. "What d'they know? They took my Jade Rose away, but I found her and brought her home. And not you nor any man is going to take her away again."

"She's going back into care," Josh said. "Away from your filthy influence."

"NO!" Jade Rose threw the kettle at Josh. "I'm not going back to my foster parents. They called me mad!"

The kettle was driven by her power. Focusing on his Da, Josh was flung across the one roomed hovel. Bright lights flickered and black threatened to wash over him.

"*Oh Lord heal me, for my bones are sore vexed,*" Josh muttered. His vision cleared.

"How did he get in?" Da demanded. "Did you forget to close the way?"

"Me!" Jade Rose shrieked. "I did it the same as ever."

With her hand she grabbed a burning log from the fire. It flared with her anger.

"Jade Rose put that back on the fire," Da's control spells slipped further.

The burning brand scorched the roof. Jade Rose took a step towards Da. He stepped towards the open door.

"Jade Rose, obey me. Put that on the fire!"

Josh used the wall to get his feet. Still unsteady, he leaned a hand against the stones. Cold wind pushed its way through the cracks.

"Josh, stop her," Da said. "She's gone mad!" His feeble attempts at control flickered towards Josh and fell short.

"I am not mad!" Jade Rose clenched her fists.

Josh raised his hands. "*Peace be within thy walls.*"

The fire on the burning brand died down.

Da straightened and he stared at Josh. The smile on his face was a war grimace. The idiot believed he had influenced Josh.

Jade Rose swung the glowing brand at Josh. He dodged out of the way. He caught her wrist and pressed. She screamed and dropped the brand. She kicked him in the knee. Josh swore, and then lifted her off her feet so her ear was next to his mouth.

"This isn't how it goes, Jade Rose," Josh whispered. "We can get him back in prison for the rest of his life."

"NO!" Jade Rose said. "If he goes away I have no one! Me Mam left and they put me in care."

"You got me, Jade," Josh said. "I'm your brother."

"You can both work for me." Da tugged on his feeble control spells.

Josh set Jade Rose on the floor. He stared at Da. He hardly needed to counter the spell, but to do so would show the man what he was dealing with.

"Draw me out of the net that they have laid for me."

The feeble spell snapped back on Da. He grabbed his head and screamed. Then he snapped his hands down. He grabbed the camping kettle and charged at Jade Rose.

Josh stuffed his foot out and tripped him.

Jade Rose's power burst out in a terrified and soundless scream.

Without his full shielding, Josh dropped to the floor, head in his hands, pushing up his barriers against her psychic attack.

He had to stop her. Forcing his way through a jelly that was entirely in his own mind he made for Jade Rose. He grabbed her and held on.

"He shall lead me forth beside the waters of comfort," he shouted.

The attack died as he clamped a mental bomb disposal dome over Jade Rose's power.

She hung in his arms crying with her power storm damped down. The storm outside drummed on the metal roof. The wind was determined to lift off the tin sheets.

Still clinging to Jade Rose, Josh check for his Da. The man hung on the gorse bush outside in the rain.

Mr. Dunkley hacked through the hedge with a sword. His fancy coat was in tatters and he was covered in cuts and scratches from the gorse but he'd got through even with the gorse injunction against witches. He stood panting, as if he had raced the last few feet.

Josh stared at him. "You knew about them."

"I found him after he'd been released on parole. When Miss Analay hides the skeletons in her past she does a thorough job. I raced to find Jade Rose and get her under our protection, but he had already taken her."

"You should have told me."

"Yes," Dunkley said. "I had no idea they were behind this or I would have left you out."

Josh cast a glance at Da who struggled to get free of the gorse. It was appropriate that the man was impaled on gorse. The other thing it stood for in folklore was the ending of complicated relationships.

"Me Da had a thing for 'J' names, huh?"

"Don't you know your father's name?"

Josh shook his head. "Me Mam removed him from my birth certificate. With a pair of scissors."

"Jonathan Dilkes, John."

"I like the way you called me Jade, not hateful Jade Rose." Jade huddled closer. "He stabbed me Mam with a kitchen knife and she got took to hospital. The council people fetched me away but she never came for me. But you can stop the madness?" She stared up at him with trusting eyes. "You can teach me to be like you?"

Josh clamped his mouth shut over the benign negatives the College required him to say. What the hell was he going to do with a little girl? Dunkley grinned at his dilemma.

But he hugged the girl closer and glared at Dunkley. "S'okay Jade, I'm your big brother. I can take care of you now."

Dancing for the Dawn

Pitkeathly followed Analay from the car park up to Stonehenge. They bypassed the Visitors' Centre, but at 11pm that was closed anyway.

"So what are we here for? I mean the 28th February is hardly occult," Pitkeathly said. "It's not even an ending this year."

Analay ignored his question and continued his even pace up the path. Above them, the iconic sarsen stones stood as they had done for millennia. An itch ran down Pitkeathly's spine from all the silence.

"*For they intended mischief against thee,*" he whispered.

There was nothing out there—except for the huge air demon bound under this henge. And an air of anticipation, expectation, hope.

Analay stopped when they crossed the outer ditch. He groped about a bit in the dark, and then crouched. "There's a long box near your feet. Find it without your torch, please: I don't want to lose my night vision. Don't open it, for that we need to be sheltered by the circle."

Analay's formality worried Pitkeathly: this wasn't the guy he went for a pint with after work.

"Soon would be nice," Analay added.

Pitkeathly swiped the area in front of him with a toe and his boot thumped against wood. He hunkered down and sketched out the edges. Wet grass brushed against his knuckles. This box was sword length.

Beside him, Analay carried a similar long box.

Fear spiked Pitkeathly's heart rate. Did he have to fight Analay? He wouldn't last two minutes against the older student, who reveled in fighting dirty to prove he was no gentleman.

"Pick up the pace, kid," Analay said. "We need to finish before midnight."

Getting a grip on his fear, Pitkeathly hefted the box onto his shoulder. Yes, it had the right weight for a sword too.

Analay strode towards the main circle and Pitkeathly trotted after him, pretending calm. They stopped between two vast standing stones, the heavy cap stone over their heads.

Setting his box on the ground, Analay shucked off his coat. Pitkeathly rested his box against the sarsen.

"So what are we doing?" Pitkeathly asked

Analay slipped on a pair of fingerless leather gloves and fastened them; the studs glinted on the back in the feeble light. "This is it, kid. Do you have what it takes to be one of the Cardinal Angels?"

"But I'm a fourth year! I've not even passed my fifth year exam."

Analay snorted. "The fifth year exam requires only your survival."

Pitkeathly rubbed at his short hair. "You've done this?"

"Yes. The test happens every four years."

Hey, at least it was survivable; minor comfort here. But… "But you'd have been a third year!"

"Oh, you can count, that's good," Analay said. "Sometimes I wonder what those posh schools teach. Tomorrow is a day that doesn't exist—the 29th February. We get to make sure it happens."

Pitkeathly leaned back on the sarsen. "This is another of those magical, mystical things I've got to take on faith, right?"

"You mean the College is a huntin', shootin' and fishin' club?" Analay mimicked a posh accent well, now he'd been at the College for seven years. "I thought we were some sort of Religious Order. Thanks for putting me straight! Duh! Pass this and you work towards ordination—a little 'faith' doesn't go amiss here."

"You're a fraud!" Analay said. "You act all bad-ass pagan but you're more religious than the lot of us."

"I never went to public school and learnt lip service hypocrisy … Kid, quit stalling, we're on a schedule."

"If I pass this do you stop calling me 'kid'?" Pitkeathly hesitated with his hands over his box. "So how do we do this … making sure tomorrow comes? Are we going to fight?"

"It's more of a sword dance." Analay opened his box.

The whole light of the Universe spilled out of the box. It sang in Pitkeathly's head, bypassing his ears.

He drove back the mind noise. First he built picket fences then vast dams to stem the silent sound.

The light flowed around him and he unclamped his hands from over his ears. In the unearthly light cast by the sword, Analay watched him. The older student wore that marble mask that so often came over the tutors when they worked with the strongest powers.

Pitkeathly gritted his teeth against his resentment. Analay knew what would happen and had been able to prepare.

But that knowledge wouldn't have been available last time when he had to take the test.

"Don't worry." Analay's voice was at the distant edge of the galaxy, but almost in Pitkeathly's head too. "We're not going to fight. These swords aren't meant for killing. I get to stand point for you, like Karl Stempress did for me four years ago."

Hands trembling, Pitkeathly slipped the catch on his box. He clung to the dykes in his head as he lifted the lid.

Dark void from the depths of space silenced the song of life. Air froze in his lungs. With conscious effort he forced his breath in and out as he patched the leaking defenses in his head.

He had no gloves so braced for impact and set his hand on the hilt.

Emptiness, loneliness filled his soul. He had frozen in place like one of these stones. One by one the stars would go out in the Universe until in the end the only thing left would be cold empty silence. And that silence sang to him. Between the impatient shuffles from Analay, he heard the grass growing, but all that would be gone. Cold, empty space filled with burnt out stars for ever and ever, Amen.

Analay spoke the truth when he asserted they wouldn't be fighting: if these two swords ever crossed, they would end the Universe.

Pitkeathly forced his eyes open and stared at the grass. It was here. It was alive.

He tore his mind away from stagnant forever.

Linked to the sword, he saw clearly in the darkness. Almost as if the song of silence was echolocation—he saw the part of every living thing that was dying. The chill of the night soaked into his skin. He sat back on his heels to stare into the black circle. Nothing moved in there.

"Are you ready yet?" Analay demanded.

"No!" Pitkeathly strived to keep the quiver of fear out of his voice. "I'm not ready for this."

"You passed the first part." Analay stepped away from the edge of the circle and leaned against the nearest upright sarsen.

"Huh?" Pitkeathly continued staring into the darkness.

"Your head didn't explode."

A boot up Pitkeathly's rear tipped him into the circle. He sprawled on the damp grass still clinging to the sword. He rolled to his knees, spluttering a swear word, while Analay laughed like a cruel god. The knees of Pitkeathly's jeans soaked through from the evening dew.

Under the sword of death and decay, the grass wilted in a sword shaped scar. He snatched the sword away from the fading grass.

Analay stepped into the circle—his sword singing of light and life.

Pitkeathly scrambled up from the wet grass prepared to fight his way through Analay to safety. The sword was going back in the box. He would never be ready for this.

With Analay's entrance, four more figures stepped out from between standing stones. By their presence they quartered the circle, standing at the cardinal compass points.

Pitkeathly's odd night sight identified them as Marishes, Mr. Kilbride, Mr. Dunkley and Karl Stempress, who had studied under Mr. Marishes. There should have been a fourth Master tutor, but Mr. Trewithick had retired from the College at the same time as his student had been dismissed for putting his long term relationship above his duty to the College.

Pitkeathly sagged. There was no point in running now. He'd hit a circle if he tried. Now the only ways out were to pass the test or die. He'd hesitated too long and now he was stuck with the results.

"I was serious about the Midnight deadline. You don't want to think about this too long," Analay said. "How about I fetch your test?"

Pitkeathly swore under his breath as Analay trotted over to the Altar stone—which was an ordinary stone that had toppled. With his eyes adjusted to the sword-enhanced sight, he saw a large figure lying across the stone—death hazed around it.

He tightened his grip on the sword hilt; his sweating palms threatened to slip the sword from his grasp. How could this be happening? He wasn't ready to be tested for this. Why had he ever aspired to belong to the Inner Circle? His Uncle on the High Council thought little of the Inner Circle—a state reciprocated by the Cardinal Angels. But any one person from the Inner Circle could wipe the High Council off the map if they wanted. Pitkeathly intended to be the best. He watched Analay and steadied his soul. One of the best at least.

Analay lifted his sword of joy and life. He touched the wrists of the prone figure and shouted, "*He delivered their power into captivity.*"

Analay bounced away as the man rolled off the Altar stone and to his feet. He glanced at Analay retreating but stayed where he was taking deep breaths.

Each breath swelled his chest like a great bellows. The chest did not deflate. Each time he inhaled the man swelled up. His muscles accepted the extra oxygen and grew.

He growled as if he were wheezing.

Pitkeathly's muscles turned to water. The Masters of the College had found a berserker, a man so attuned to his spirit he exerted control over his transformations. Usually a bear or wolf spirit inhabited the body. Vikings knew how to control berserker spirits— a skill lost with the defeat of the pagans.

If Pitkeathly let the man reach his full transformation he had no chance of defeating him. The Sword of decay slid in his sweaty palms. He settled his grip and pushed off. He rushed in to take out the creature.

The berserker lifted its head and saw its nemesis charging. It jumped up onto the Altar stone. Its feet clattered on the stone, not like the pads of a wolf or a bear.

The man clawed at his temples and grunted with pain. Horns forced their way out of the berserker's head. What was that about?

Pitkeathly pounded in; from this angle he could take out the legs.

The creature leapt from the stone over his head and landed on the ground. It charged to the edge of the circle and bounced off the spiritual wall the tutors held in place.

Unfazed, it stared at Pitkeathly, first one eye then the other getting a fix on its enemy's location. With full horns now, Pitkeathley recognized the creature; the Masters had found a bull spirit, which made its possessor into a Minotaur.

Was it a fair test if the creature was not native to this country? It must have arrived with immigrants from Crete.

The creature lowered its head and barreled towards Pitkeathly.

He dived out of the way and rolled to his feet, keeping the creature in sight.

Analay engaged the creature. The horns sparked as they hit the Sword of life. Pitkeathly admired the way he fended off the attack. Even with Analay's prior knowledge of what they'd be facing his fighting skills made the job look easy.

A double aura hung about the creature; no time to worry about that. Pitkeathly crowded in, prepared to skewer the Minotaur.

The creature dodged and clumped around the altar stone.

No! Analay was right in the path of Pitkeathly's sword. The older student was about to be spit roast. The Sword of destruction sang in soundless delight as it bore down on the Sword of light.

Analay whisked his Sword away and fended off the other Sword with the knuckledusters on his off hand.

"Have a care, Pitkeathly." Analay danced to one side.

Hands on hips, the creature snorted with bull-ly laughter as it watched Pitkeathly's cock-up.

No time to sag in relief at Analay's casual skill. He needed to be a Witch-Finder, not a man holding a sword.

"*I will take no bullock out of thine house. The beasts of the Forest are mine and so are the cattle upon a thousand hills.*"

The spell should tame a wild beast and hold it still for slaughter, but the words slid off the creature—as if it wore a second skin.

Alerted by the spell, the creature lowered its horns and charged Pitkeathly.

He waited until the last minute and threw himself to one side. His trainers skidded in the dew and he landed on his backside.

As he rolled to his feet, the Minotaur rammed its horns on the Altar stone. The creature staggered back. On his feet, Pitkeathly circled the beast.

"*With my whole heart I have sought thee.*" He stared at the Minotaur. He was right; two spirits controlled the beast.

Follow the lines of power, hey?

The creature roared and charged him.

Running for his life, he had to let his spell go. He vaulted the Altar stone and landed on the other side.

What was happening here?

This was the test, not the slaughter of the beast. His tutors were keen on saving people despite the misery exorcism caused.

"*Open thou mine eyes, that I may view the wondrous things of thy law.*"

He raced around the Altar stone, away from the Minotaur that circled the stone.

The top creature controlling the Minotaur was the bull spirit powering the berserker change. Underneath another, larger, spirit lurked. He kept the Altar stone between him and the Minotaur and again he followed the power.

He gasped. The power led straight down. The huge air elemental, trapped under Stonehenge, fed power and protection to the Minotaur.

Now he was in deep shit.

And there was a huge flaw in the retention spell that kept the spirit trapped under Stonehenge. An elemental that vast was beyond the power of an ordinary person to defeat. Yet, if he failed the demon would escape through the flaw and destroy the whole of England. So that was why Analay had hinted this battle involved more than personal survival.

So there had to be another way.

What did he have? A sword that promoted death and decay, a person on point with a sword that promoted life and growth, and knowledge.

He continued holding the Altar stone between himself and the Minotaur while he planned.

The spirit infesting the bull creature must be a water elemental. He reversed direction as the Minotaur raced the other way. This was a circle designed to hold an air elemental.

The bull leapt up on the Altar stone and raced across.

Pitkeathly threw himself at the altar stone as the Minotaur jumped down on him. He raised the Sword as he flew underneath the beast. The bull raged as the tip of the Sword sliced across its hip. Blood ran down the blade. The metal sucked it in as the Sword sang a vast dirge that filled the Universe—almost deafening all his senses. Could he kill the Minotaur with the sword?

Gathering his wits, Pitkeathly wiped the blade on his jeans. It muted the death march the sword was singing.

As he cleaned the sword, the Minotaur's limp faded away. It aimed its horns at him. The bull spirit that infested the creature could heal even a cut by this Sword when fed extra power by the spirit trapped in the henge. The creature raced towards Pitkeathly.

He stayed crouched until the last second. He surged up, using the muscles in his legs to drive the sword through the Minotaur.

The creature angled away and the sword slid into the top of the shoulder. The edge cut its way out. The creature's left arm flopped as if he had slit the controlling tendons.

It bellowed and staggered away into Analay's path.

Analay thumped it with the knuckledusters on his off hand.

The creature crumpled, a hand held to its nose.

Instead of finishing it Analay backed away and lifted a questioning eyebrow at Pitkeathly, leaving the younger student to finish the business. Pitkeathly raised his sword to lop off its head.

A memory stopped him. What else had Analay revealed? '*These swords aren't meant for killing.*' Pitkeathly glanced at Analay who remained impassive.

He had to do something, and quickly as the beast spirit was already repairing the damage done to the body.

Why shouldn't he kill the creature?

Because he had nothing into which to bind the spirit as it was released. This was a circle to bind air elementals not water demons. If he killed the spirit's current host, the spirit would jump to the nearest possible container—which with Analay standing back was Pitkeathly.

Pitkeathly drew away from the creature. He saw Analay nod. He had to deal with the demon without killing, and soon.

The position of the stars showed Midnight creeping closer. The air elemental anticipated its escape.

He had no container to house an elemental. What did he have?

An air elemental helping a water elemental was not unheard of, but a difficult combination to counter.

Opposites. That's what the swords were and that's what he needed here. Fire opposed water, but withdrawal of air would kill it too. Earth opposed air but was drowned by water. So not only opposites but all the elements were needed here. What if there was burning earth that promoted death and life?

What he needed was a volcano. It killed immediately but volcanic ash was the most fertile. Opening up a volcano in the middle of Salisbury plain with himself in ground zero was a stupid thing to do. Not to mention the cathedral city of Salisbury less than ten miles away.

A more localized disaster was needed.

No! That would still kill the creature. There had to be some way to bind the bull spirit to stop the spirit leaping to another host. And soon: it was almost midnight.

He needed water to bind it into and hadn't even brought a bottle of mineral water with him. The bull bellowed, its head swinging this way and that to bring him into focus. Getting its hooves settled tried to get up, and slipped on grass. The fur on the bull clumped into rat's tails.

Because they were wet.

Pitkeathly's mouth dropped open. There was water here, the sort you never notice. The grass was covered in droplets of dew.

Now he knew what to do. Pitkeathly darted to the downed bull and drew his blade over the bull's forearm.

A bellow roared out over the henge. The sword of decay must sting more than most blades. Blood dripped onto the grass.

"My soul is athirst for God."

The bull tried to get to its hooves again, but staggered, weakened as the bull spirit leaked out of the man's body with the blood. The red droplets beaded on the grass like dew. The Minotaur became a shrieking man as the bones and flesh shrank back into true form without the buffering of the spirit. Bruises sprang up all over his body. He rolled in the grass and tried to slurp up the blood and the bull spirit with it.

Pitkeathly kicked the man aside and laid his sword of decay over the grass. *"For they shall be cut down like the grass and be withered even as the green herb."*

The grass grew brown and lifeless under the sword blade.

The former Minotaur wept as he ran at Pitkeathly's sword intending to impale himself.

Analay rested the Sword of Life on the man's back.

"Heaviness may endure for a night, but joy cometh in the morning." The man dropped into sleep. "Thought for a minute there I was going to have to sort it out."

"So why today? Why is midnight today the weakness in the binding?"

"Because the 29th February isn't a real day, it wasn't taken into account in the original binding. So every four years we have to make the day real by symbolically defeating the air demon again, by proxy."

Sweat ran down Pitkeathly's back. "We have to do that every four years? Why not rebind it?"

"Check out what that would take some time, and ask yourself if we have enough people—we're down one of the Cardinal Angels. But hey, you did great. Welcome to the Inner Circle."

Wind tore across the open hills. It wuthered around the sarsen stones. The four men guarding the circle raised their staffs. Pitkeathly only heard their chant, not the words.

Midnight fell over Salisbury Plain. The wind carried the sound of a bell tolling twelve times. Gales howled the air elemental's disappointment across the whole of Salisbury plain. Inside the circle not even a breeze stirred the grass as the strong capped sarsens held the air elemental bound.

Scouting for Girls

Le-ann Hopshort was dragged into the scout hut, her mother's hand pressing on her shoulder. Mrs. Cutcheon, the vicar's wife, strode over, her Mary Jane shoes tapping on the bare wood floor.

"Dear Eleanor, I'm so glad you decided to join us," Mrs. Cutcheon said.

"I'm called Le-ann."

"I'm sure she'll enjoy it. Won't you, Le-ann?" Mrs. Hopshort gave a sharp shake to her daughter's shoulder and leaned close to her ear. "You know I need five minutes peace, so behave."

"I was supposed to be studying my science tonight, not earning a sewing badge at Girly Guides," Le-ann muttered.

Mrs. Cutcheon took Le-ann's hand. "And you know, dear, you will study better for taking a break and doing something else. Don't worry, Mrs. Hopshort, I'm sure El… I mean Le-ann will find something in the 2nd Helmsley Company to keep her occupied for one evening."

"I've got to rush away; my neighbor's babysitting Matthew for half an hour. He's got this dreadful measles, you know." Le-ann's mother hurried away.

Le-ann let Mrs. Cutcheon lead her into the scout hut. At least this way she was clear of *The Parent* for the evening. She needed to make this work for her. In all there were ten other girls in the scout hut, divided into two groups.

Mrs. Cutcheon had walked up to the group of five girls sitting in the back corner. The leader was Ariella Gooders—a girl determined to be good at everything.

"Ari, you'll be Le-ann's friend for the evening, won't you?" Mrs. Cutcheon said.

"Of course." Ariella eyed Le-ann as Mrs. Cutcheon trotted away. "You bragged all day about the invitation about joining Mr. Draper's evening study group."

"I should be there," Le-ann hissed. "But Mrs. Cutcheon grabbed my mother's ear and told her all sorts of lies."

"Depends on what Mrs. Cutcheon told her."

"You're envious you didn't get the invite."

Ariella gazed at Le-ann from under lowered lids. "I got one last year. I declined. This is so much more fun. Here, wear this for tonight anyway."

Ariella handed Le-ann a pin badge enameled with a white heather sprig. All the girls in this group wore them. Le-ann gritted her teeth and pinned it onto her tee shirt.

Mrs. Cutcheon stood in the center of the room and clapped her hands. "Right girls, first things first, let's get on with the fairy cakes for the Church Social after the 11am Sunday Service."

Le-ann spluttered. "This is fun?"

"Depends on what you make of it," Ariella whispered. "And the sewing badge taught me a great deal." She tapped a small circle of cloth on her sleeve depicting a rag doll.

Mrs. Cutcheon frowned at Ariella. "Let's start the evening with the baking prayer. Put your hearts into it girls."

Around Le-ann the girls bowed their heads and folded their hands together. Girls Le-ann had met in other circumstance—like Jade Analay who was fostered by Mr. and Mrs. Cutcheon and was rumored to have been in juvenile detention for arson. Well, Le-ann had seen her smoking round the back of the bike sheds at school. There was Courtney who shagged anything and Megan who had cut off her plait to bury it when her pet rabbit died—all of them dressed in knee-length blue shorts and lemon yellow shirts straight out of a 1950s adventure book for girls. Ariella, standing there pious as all hell, dyed her hair black and dressed like the Corpse Bride out of school. Tonight, she plaited her long hair in a tail down her back and had a center parting.

Such hypocrisy, sucking up to the vicar's wife. Why would any of them bother? Helmsley High School wasn't Church of England funded.

"Let us pray. Dear Lord, Thou the bread of angels, graciously deign to bless our baking *that all who partake of it may have health of body* and soul. Who livest and reignest for ever and ever. Amen."

They put some odd stresses in the prayer. Le-ann didn't trouble to work them out. After the prayer, Ariella took her back to the corner with her group.

"Le-ann, you know most of us." Ariella pointed at the fifth girl who wore a lemon yellow hairband holding her auburn hair out of her eyes. "But Fenny here—that's Fenella Pitkeathly for formal—slums it with us plebs from her private girls' school over near Easingwold."

"One feels that the Guides here are more interesting than the company in one's school." Fenny parodied her own posh accent.

Courtney sniggered and batted Fenny on the arm. All the girls bent to cupboards and retrieved mixing bowls and dishes. Mrs. Cutcheon left a basket of ingredients with each patrol.

"Get a wiggle on," Ariella said. "If we get our cakes in the oven first, you lot can work on your sewing badges." She cast a mischievous glance at Le-ann. The other four girls giggled—even emo Megan.

Le-ann found a chair and sank into it to watch the others.

"Hi, you!" Ariella waved an arm in front of her face.

"What?"

"As the newcomer you get to set out the paper bun cases in the tray." Ariella handed Le-ann a packet of cases, white ones with little red crosses printed over them. Oh yes, these were for the church social.

"Oh joy!" Le-ann scooted her chair closer to the table and set out paper cases in each of five trays.

On the other side of the table the girls muttered. They acted like were rehearsing Macbeth instead of baking. Courtney's blonde bob splayed out around her head as if she'd used the cake mixture as hair gel.

Soon the girls were dolloping their mixture into the paper cases.

"Quick, Poppy Patrol are nearly done," Ariella said.

Some of the cake mix spilled out over the tray. Fenny ran a finger through it and licked it. Ariella swiped her hand and the patrol picked up their trays piled into the scout hall kitchen before the other Patrol.

Ariella grinned at Jade. "Go on. You light the oven. You know you want to."

Jade sniggered. She opened an oven. Le-ann missed what happened next because she was eyeing up the back door, but heat roiled out of the open oven and all the girls were laughing.

"Maybe a bit more control next time, Jade." Ariella giggled.

Where were Jade's matches?

White heather patrol slid their cakes into the oven. Now, here was her chance.

"Ari, I need to go to the loo," Le-ann said.

"Sure, it's over by the back door. Come back in when you're ready." Indifferent, Ariella gathered to the rest of White Heather Patrol. "Who brought their poppets?"

"I did." "Me!" "Of course!"

Le-ann darted through the door marked 'ladies'. With her ear pressed to the door, she heard their feet tippy-tap in their sandshoes back into the main hall.

Fast as possible she slipped over to the door. It was unlocked! She had expected to be penned in. She slipped out of the scout hall. She was free! Mr. Draper's study group waited for her.

She ran over the gravel of the scout hut car park. It wasn't far to the school. She ran all the way, freedom lending wings to her feet. Night crept up on the town, lengthening the shadows while the sky was still bright.

She had beaten her mother and that silly Mrs. Cutcheon.

The school gates were open as she arrived and ghost lights lit up the empty classrooms for security. She circled the school, round behind the bike shed and on towards her beacon, the downstairs science labs. In the shadow of the school buildings, it was almost dark. The windows of L3 glowed red around the edge of the blinds.

Le-ann tapped on the glass. Georgia's face appeared when the blind lifted.

The window opened. "It's Le-ann, Master Draper."

"That's brilliant." Mr. Draper appeared at the window. "Can you climb in?"

Le-ann jumped and got a knee up on the windowsill. Using that as leverage she hauled the leg inside the window. As she straddled the window ledge she took in changes to her usual classroom. On the teacher's bench stood a cauldron over a portable gas stove. It gave off an intense heat.

Georgia pulled Le-ann all the way in. She wafted her face with the air from outside, and lowered the blind before Mr. Draper saw what she did. "Come on, it's great here. You'll love it."

The girls all wore black lab coats tied with sashes covered in a various colored stars.

"I thought we were revising our chemistry," Le-ann said.

Mr. Draper hooked an arm around her shoulder. "In a way we are, my dear, but the chemistry we're revising is a bit earlier than you expected."

"We're learning Alchemy," Marilee burst out.

"The real deal?" Le-ann asked.

"Most definitely," Mr. Draper said. "Rikki guide our newest sorceress."

Rikki hooked an arm through Le-ann's and dragged her away from peering into the pot. It contained a dirty liquid, which was heating up. This was better than a cookery badge any day.

"Prepare the ingredients to our potion."

"Yes, Master Draper." The girls chorused and Le-ann joined in.

"Rikki, fit our newest recruit with proper robes."

Rikki tugged on her arm. "Our cupboard is over here. Master Draper keeps it locked during school hours."

She rummaged in the cupboard brought a black coat for Le-ann who tugged it on over her jeans and tee shirt. She fitted in better now.

Rikki handed her a sash. "You have a gray sash because you are a novice. Once you're initiated you get a black sash like ours and can earn your constellation." She tapped on the stars.

Le-ann wrapped the sash around her waist determined to be initiated as soon as possible. This was way cooler than lemon yellow shirts and blue shorts.

"So what's in the pot?"

"That's water from a puddle that has had dog poo in it. Master Draper brought that. Come over here, and we'll prepare our part of the ingredients."

"What do I do?"

"Chop this onion, and let your tears fall onto the minced veg." Rikki handed Le-ann a knife and an onion.

To one side Georgia let out an explosive sneeze. "How much more do I have to grind this pepper, Master Draper?"

"Finer than dust," he said. "Marilee, I gave you the hard part this week. Last week Georgia found us a bat. So what have you managed to get for us this week?"

Through tear streaked eyes Le-ann peered at Marilee.

Marilee lifted up a jam jar. "I collected all these silverfish. My granny's kitchen is swarming with them."

The little insects squirmed and wriggled. Le-ann hoped she wouldn't have to touch them.

Mr. Draper nodded. "They'll do, my dear. Right everyone, bring your prepared ingredients to the cauldron. It's boiling at Fever pitch."

Le-ann carried her onion to the cauldron with Rikki.

Mr. Draper pointed at Rikki and Le-ann. "Onion for the watery swollen eyes."

The two girls dropped their load into the boiling water.

"Pepper, for sneezing."

Georgia tipped the contents of her pestle and mortar into the cauldron.

"Silverfish for photophobia."

Marilee, who wore her blonde hair in two pony tails while in school, tipped the jam jar of still squirming insects into the boiling water.

Le-ann glanced around the circle, but no one else was disturbed by dropping live creatures into boiling water.

"Take these ice lumps in your hands and hold them until your finger joints ache. Once you can no longer stand the pain, drop the ice cube and your pain into the cauldron."

Le-ann accepted her lump of ice and cupped her hand around it. "What are we doing here?"

Rikki eyes were alight with pleasure. "Why, we're increasing the strength of the measles epidemic."

"What!" Le-ann dropped her ice on the floor.

"Oh tut! Le-ann. You'll have to try again with fresh," Mr. Draper said.

"But my brother has measles. My mum is so worried, the doctor says he's getting pneumonia."

"So this week we'll learn better focus, girls," Mr. Draper said. "We don't want any of the deaths in our families do we?"

Le-ann backed away from the gathering around the gas stove. "Are you mad?"

Georgia gasped and dropped her ice into the cauldron. "Ah! That hurts!"

Rikki and Marilee stood with agony lining their faces, determined not to be the one to give in first.

Mr. Draper shook his head. "You wanted to join in my chemistry study group. What's wrong now?"

"But if my brother gets any worse the doctor insisted he'll have to go to hospital. He might die! How can you do this?"

"My sorceresses need the practice if they're going to be any good. Don't you want to be the best, Le-ann? We're so lucky that uptake of the vaccination has been so poor. Science is the blight of modern sorcery."

"I don't want this."

Rikki dropped the ice cube into the cauldron. "What are you talking about? This is life!"

Marilee chucked her ice into the cauldron. "Not sorceress material, hey? Her brother has the measles so when she catches the virus everyone will be expecting it."

Marilee caught up the ladle and scooped liquid from the cauldron. She chucked it in Le-ann's face.

"Oh dear," Mr. Draper said. "That was more than a lethal dose. We need to spread it out in a mist over the town."

Le-ann's eyes burned and the room became hot and stuffy. She staggered over to the window, to let more air in. Her throat blistered. She fell against the wall and sagged to the floor. Why had she wanted to come here? Even baking fairy cakes with the Girl Guides sounded more fun than cooking up illnesses.

Ariella burst in through the open window followed by Courtney, who hauled on the blind cord to open it.

"You!" Mr. Draper shouted. "*Biber verinenum in auro.*"

Le-ann saw a cloud of darkness surge towards Ariella.

"Oooooo! You swore!" Ariella giggled. "*Let them be confounded that are against my soul.*"

A golden light bit away at the darkness.

Fenny dropped to floor near Le-ann, who coughed weakly. Her skin burnt and the even the faint light coming in through the window made her eyes ache.

"You need a fairy cake." Fenny held up one of the cakes last seen going into the oven. She peeled it out of the case and crumbled it, posting the bits into Le-ann's swollen mouth.

Courtney lifted a hand and pointed at Marilee. *"Thou hast a mighty arm."*

Marilee jerked backwards, as if someone had hit her.

Ariella clapped. "Oh! Good one, Court!"

"How about this one, Ari?" Megan pointed at Rikki then at Georgia. *"I shall smite down his foes before his face.*

Both girls she indicated fell to the floor.

Courtney glowered. "That's showing off."

As Le-ann swallowed bits of fairy cake the blistering in her mouth and throat vanished. As her watery, swollen eyes cleared she saw Jade creeping around the back of the classroom while Ariella distracted Mr. Draper. Ariella acted like she was holding back on her abilities.

Behind the teacher's bench, Jade switched off the gas. She toppled the cauldron. Liquid splattered everyone on that side of the room.

Mr. Draper leapt to the top of a teaching bench, leaving his sorceresses to their fate. *"Pulvis et Umbra Sumus!"*

The Dark cloud he had sent after Ariella spread tentacles out to catch all of White Heather Patrol.

Ariella watched as the tendrils reached for her friends. She took a rag doll out of her pocket. "Of course, I've passed my sewing badge." She winked at Le-ann as she pulled a needle out of her shirt collar. "Here's one I made earlier. *Away from me ye wicked."*

She stabbed at the poppet's arm.

Mr. Draper clutched at his right arm. He muttered something, but Ariella stabbed his other elbow and wiggled the needle.

Le-ann had never heard a grown man scream in agony. Ariella held the poppet up and showed him where the next needle strike would be. He curled in anticipation, with his hands cupping his groin.

"Ariella!" Mrs. Cutcheon said. "More lady-like please. What are you girls doing out here?"

White Heather patrol came to attention.

"Field trip, Mrs. Cutcheon. You indicated you wanted us to recruit Le-ann. So we're showing her what we do." Behind her back she waved the entire patrol to the window. Fenny helped Le-ann to her feet.

Mr. Draper uncurled and lifted a hand.

"Watch out," Le-ann shouted.

Ariella spun and stabled the needle through his leg, leaving it in place. Mr. Draper fell off the teacher's bench and splat into the measles mixture.

"White Heather patrol, regroup outside please," Ariella said.

Jade leapt out of the window, followed by Courtney. Megan helped Fenny with Le-ann. Last of all, Ariella climbed out of the window.

"Nice poppet work, there, Ariella," Mrs. Cutcheon said. "You're ready to take your craftwork badge. Fenny, good in-field first aid. And I shall recommend White Heather patrol for their emergency response badges. Well done."

Le-ann stripped off the black lab coat and dumped it on the ground outside the lab window. "How did you find me?" she whispered to Fenny.

Fenny flicked the White Heather badge on her tee shirt with a fingernail. "Didn't I say this company was interesting?"

Mrs. Cutcheon flapped about like a hen with her chicks, ushering the guides out of the school grounds and heading towards the scout hut.

"Was all that magic?" she said.

"Oh no," Ariella said. "*They* were doing magic, but we countered them using Practical Theology. Mrs. Cutcheon persuaded Jade's very reverend brother to show us how."

"My brother's one of the Church Militant." Jade sniggered.

"Will I get to learn all this if I join Girl Guides?"

Mrs. Cutcheon patted her shoulder. "Oh yes, you're the sort of girl we hope to recruit into our little troop. But we keep it to ourselves, and promise never to talk about it outside of our circle."

They reached the scout hut, as the meeting came to an end. Mrs. Cutcheon led the closing prayers. "And remember, girls, we have Mr. Analay visiting next week to teach us some more of the 'special prayers'."

"If he remembers where he left his dog collar," Jade muttered. Ariella flicked her arm.

As the meeting broke up Ariella took Le-ann to where her mother waited at the door.

"Mum. I want to do this every week. We made cakes."

"Wait until you learn what you have to do for the astronomy badge." Ariella touched a patch on her sleeve.

Mrs. Hopshort stared at her daughter, then at Mrs. Cutcheon.

"It's the way we present the material." Mrs. Cutcheon handed Le-ann one of White Heather patrol's fairy cakes. "You'll want to take a cake for your little brother, Le-ann. Just the sort of treat he'll like if he's under the weather."

Le-ann accepted the cake and joined her mother in the car. Yeah! She wanted to get her cookery badge.

Books by Vanessa Knipe

A DATE WITH DARKNESS*
HARD LESSONS*
SHADOW AND SALVATION*
WITCH-FINDER*

*ST. VAN HELSING THEOLOGICAL COLLEGE